JUAN DE LA COSA / JOHN OF THE THING

A TABLE MADE AGAIN FOR THE FIRST TIME

ON
KATE BRIGGS'
THIS LITTLE ART

INDEX

EDITORS' NOTE

... though we are not really editors in the true sense; neither of us arrive with any formal training, but as readers first and foremost and as artists working at a shared intersection between writing/literature and image-making. In other words, passionately interested amateurs.

This publication has arisen directly from the spirit of artistic, literary and critical enquiry set forth in the British writer and translator Kate Briggs' unprecedented *This Little Art* (Fitzcarraldo Editions, 2017). Hannah Arendt said of the best sort of storytelling, that it 'reveals meaning without committing the error of defining it.' The revelations in TLA are to be found in the book's intensely discursive, reflective nature and in the series of essential questions it raises for us. The spirit of open-hearted enquiry continued to play out and ramify between us, to the extent that we both felt there was more business here to be done.

The definition of artist is not at its most interesting in terms of the *virtuosic*: the professional, the person who knows what they are doing; because as the virtuoso arrives, so the possibilities of art making seem to crumble away and both the lone, male genius and the academy loom depressingly into view. Positions of arrival, complete understanding and finality are much less interesting than the gap between thought and expression, learning as you go, *becoming* (i.e. what Kate, via Helen Lowe-Porter, describes as the *would-be* writer). This then, for us was the starting point, this generosity of being afforded such immediate access to a thinker's thinking, an openness that seems to exist in many of the greatest artworks across all forms of expression. As viewers or readers we are allowed in and are obliged to continue: to discuss as honestly, to critique as rigorously, to debate as generously.

We wanted the publication to not refer back to the book, but to utilise it as a critical starting point, a table to be shared. So that rather than being about *This Little Art,* it could serve as a space around which to gather and to try and engender something of what the book engenders. Firstly, we organised a traditional Q & A with Kate and a group of interested writers and artists who formulated their own questions, not always directly related to translation but all of them tangents emerging from the generous, discursive nature of the book. Secondly, we asked those participants to move on from the responses and the points they originally raised, expanding outwards into their own footnotes of thinking, through their various practices and positions. Finally, we have tried to move the conversation out into the world by asking a small group of external interlocutors to offer a further expansion, a beginning in the form of an ending, an afterword that could serve as a prologue, the potential groundwork for the iteration of these discussions.

Sometimes, over the past year, it has felt like this table was all we had to cling to. Heartfelt thanks to Kate and all contributors.

Paul Becker / Francesco Pedraglio

A Table Made Again for the First Time -
a collective discussion with Kate Briggs

Bureau des Réalités, Bruxelles
September 2018

PART 1

FRANCESCO PEDRAGLIO:

My first realisation while reading Kate's book was that I could not possibly do this Q & A on my own. I felt that the book presents us with so many layers, opens so many doors from which to access Kate's reasoning that I needed to open up the discussion to a larger group of people. I simply could not restrict it to Kate and I. There were so many elements I would have liked to touch upon during our chat could have been developed into further questions. And so many other elements I did not have enough time or sensitivity enough to formulate. I just felt that in doing this alone I would have missed out on too much.

Now, I realise how all these uncomfortable feelings are exactly what Kate was talking about when discussing translation as a continuous group activity. But that realisation came afterwards, as they usually do. So, I invited a few other participants to help share thoughts and ideas around this complex endeavour; artists and writers who I knew were very close to Kate and to her book. I asked them not just to provide questions, but to come along, participate actively in the discussion and bring material that they thought was interesting in reflecting upon their own work and Kate's.

Yes, some of these people are here tonight. And I did receive quite a bit of material... mostly pages and comments. Because most of the invited guests said they couldn't give me a straight question for Kate, for the same reasons I could not interview her alone. But somehow, once again, within the impossibility of summarising all the ideas in one or two questions lies a large part of the overall discussion I wanted to have with Kate. So, what I propose tonight is that I kick off the event. I have a series of questions and elucidations, and I guess some of you here haven't yet read the book...

LILOU VIDAL:
Maybe we should present the people you invited?

FP:
Oh yes, sure. So, we have artist and writer Paul Becker; artist Nadia Hebson; writer Natasha Soobramanien; writer Brenda Lozano; and finally, writer Daniela Cascella. Obviously, the artist Tania Pérez Córdova, co-editor of Juan de la Cosa / John of the Thing also heavily contributed to this event. This is the group. And there are points during the night when I know these people will want to jump in, because the comments I will present are actually theirs, and they will be able to develop them in more depth. But this is also open to anyone else in the room, whether or not you have read the book.

I'd like to start from the way the reader of *This Little Art* – me, you, anyone – can follow a series of parallel and interconnected stories all at once: there is the 'Kate Briggs story', namely the story of your relationship with your translation of Roland Barthes' final lectures at the Collège de France[1]. There is your relationship and take on your everyday life... for instance your Saturday morning gym routine. There is your relationship with writing and reading, their correspondence and also their differences. Then there are points in the book where you are fully focused on Barthes himself, his last years, his life and writing habits. There are a couple of very interesting stories about two other translators, female translators: Helen Lowe-Porter, translator of Thomas Mann, and Dorothy Bussy, friend and translator of André Gide, with whom she has also a very in-depth epistolary exchange

1. Roland Bathes, *The Preparation of the Novel*, translated into English by Kate Briggs, Columbia University Press, 2011

you so interestingly analyse. And finally there are a lot of other little sub-plots and stories bubbling up here and there, introduced, left hanging, then re-emerging a few chapters later.

I was very interested in your process of writing, since all the elements in the book are intertwined: you present the story of Thomas Mann and Helen Lowe-Porter at the beginning but we get a real historical overview of it only in the middle of the book. And all the other components are intertwined from chapter to chapter, never fully disclosing an idea of the overall issue at stake. Was yours a linear process of writing?

For a while I wondered if this could have been a book that one could read non-linearly. Is this anything that you thought about?

KATE BRIGGS:
I knew for a long time that I wanted to read a book about translation. But what kind of book? This was the question. I was reading a lot of books of translation theory, but I felt that I couldn't find any representation of my own experience in there. My own complicated, sometimes ambivalent, experience. So, I wanted to find a way of giving translation its complication, to give translation all of its complexity and its situatedness as a practice. To do so, it seemed obvious to me that I needed to start from where I was translating from. Funnily enough, I don't know whether every translator feels that the work they're dealing with speaks directly to their practice – but that was strikingly the case for me with Roland Barthes' last lecture course, *La Préparation du roman,* which I translated and which is all about the process of 'coming to write', how a person might establish the conditions of possibility for themselves to begin writing. In his case, he was talking about the project of a novel that wasn't then realised. For me, engaging in translation was also, always, about coming to write, about

understanding what writing even is, or what it could be for me – it was a means of undergoing an apprenticeship in writing. It was clear that there was so much going on in Barthes, in this lecture course but also the earlier one, *Comment vivre ensemble*, which is about being with others, living together with others, that related to the questions and gestures of translation – I felt there was my practice and then the works I was translating, and they seemed to be speaking really quite directly to one another. But of course, translation is this vast, vast question and a vast, vast field of differentiated activity. You listed some of the stories in the book, Francesco. And it's true I'm writing about the question of a novel written in German and translated into English in a particular historical moment; and then I'm writing about me translating in my own way, which results in another particular and unique kind of pairing. I have always found this idea that we can talk about translation in general quite problematic, since translation is always a relation: to talk about it means talking about more than one language, more than one situation, different bodies of work, different bodies of people. And these relations that are each time produced are sort of unreproducible, certainly ungeneralisable. It's a different thing to move from German into English than it is from French into English, and a different thing too to move in the other direction. It's different to translate Barthes into English than into German, for example. All the general things you can say about those moves, what they have in common, are quite quickly exhausted. That's why I realised that I needed to start out from where I was, and it is also the reason why there are all these different layers of stories of the book – it is because I decided to only use the materials I had to hand. That was how I could give myself permission to start. For instance, I was reading a lot of books in order to translate Barthes' lectures. One of them was *The Magic Mountain,* which led me to Helen Lowe-Porter. Another was André Gide's *Judge Not,* which led me to Dorothy Bussy, his life-long translator. And I thought that since I cannot speak to everything, since I cannot approach translation in general or for some generalising perspective – and for many deeply held reasons I don't want to – I would only work with, or at least only start from, what was already on or near my desk. So probably for the reader it feels as though the book ranges all over the place, but there was a kind of inner logic to why *these* books and *these* materials and not others. They were what I had to hand and what I had to hand led me towards, once I started thinking and reading with them. And likewise, what I also had to hand, then as now, was my own life, my day-to-day experience away from my desk, but that still accompanied the practice of translation. And as I was living, I was also thinking. So, that's why you read about me going to aerobics. That's why my kids also appear occasionally. I suppose I was trying to show how the questions I was interested in didn't stop being interesting, or relevant, in the times of day when I wasn't reading books, or thinking in the library. They mattered to me and related to other parts of life as well.

FP:
It's interesting to see how a good part of it all comes from your research on Barthes. Speaking to Paul Becker yesterday, he mentioned that you've been talking about the idea of 'form' as an important part of a discussion around your book. It's not really a concept you find in the book but once I started looking at how you ended up organising the text it suddenly became a possible question. I mean, I was trying to imagine how to structure this evening, and when Paul mentioned it I thought it was an interesting point to make. Maybe I should pass this to Paul himself.

PAUL BECKER:
Well, this book means a lot to me. One of the things that I found really interesting is that it seems to exist in lots of different areas in lots of different ways. It was difficult to pinpoint exactly what I was

reading. It felt like criticism, but sometimes it drifted into a version of autofiction, then memoir. And the list goes on. I'm wondering how were you thinking in terms of form? Or were you thinking about this at all?

KB:

One of the things that people notice is there is a lot of white space. This is one way of answering your question. If you imagine: I had this vast territory, the territory of what a translation practice is and does, and I needed to make it local to me somehow. One solution was to work and think with the books and stories I already had to hand. Another I found was to massively reduce the margins on Word so I was left on each with a very small space, so it didn't feel endless. I know that sounds funny – but it's true! I needed to scale the territory down. Because, a question that I am still wondering about: what is not relevant to translation? What would not be pertinent to a discussion about translation? Translation raises questions about identity, repetition, representation, reproduction, responsibility, ethics, politics – it's life! So, I needed to localise my zone of inquiry and I did this in one way by making a smaller space onscreen. And then I found that it is more manageable to write in these slightly smaller, delimited sections. Initially it wasn't important to me to include the Kate Briggs story. My friend Natasha Soobramanien was really crucial in this aspect. She read a first draft early on that was all about tables, quite early on I was interested in proposing an analogy between writing a translation and making a table on a desert island for the first time, Robinson Crusoe style. As in: doing something again for the first time. Making something that exists in the world already, made by someone else, and what it is to do it yourself for the first time with new materials and in a necessarily new context. Having, by necessity, to invent your own new manner of remaking what already exists. *Robinson Crusoe* was another book I had on my desk, to hand, because Barthes writes about it at some length in *Comment vivre ensemble*. I felt the analogy was a kind of thought experiment — I wanted to analyse the consequences of my analogy until I had exhausted them, to see how far the analogy would get me or to what degree I could open it up. But then I was writing it all in this mode which was very depersonalised. Natasha noted this, and I remember her asking: *Where are you in all this? It seems like you're buried in the footnotes.* I remember receiving this as a kind of provocation. Kind of: You want some of me? Really? Sure? Okay... So I sat down and wrote the scene of me walking with one of my children, pushing an empty pushchair. That released something. And of course, now there's a lot of me in the book. But although I let that scene in, I didn't want mine to be the only story of translation practice. To come back to the shorter pieces and the white space, both were tools for setting different scenes or stories in relation to each other. I wanted to set things in motion and put out things in the air, to set them provisionally down on one page and then leave them in such a way that I could return to them later on, sometimes much later on in the book. There was then a question about how many things it is actually possible to set in motion and hold together while also holding a reader with you, holding her attention – without exasperating this same reader. But to come finally to your question about form – most crucially, most vitally, I wanted to find a form that felt open – open to the reader, open to the world. And mobile...

FP:
So, from what you're saying, it seems that you wrote thinking about suspension and movement from one part to another?

KB:
Yes, absolutely. There was a lot happening around this in the final edits. I'm really interested in pace, in moments of acceleration and

slowing down and how these can be achieved in the sentence and on the page. I was trying to think about argumentation in terms of pace. Or maybe more ambitiously, I was trying to make an argument, to pursue a set of questions with the kind of narrative tension, and energy, and attentiveness to questions of pace that you tend to find in other kinds of writing – novels, for example. I think it's very easy to say things fast about translation, too fast – so fast they sound easy, or simple, and I wanted to do the opposite. I wanted to slow down and unpack and take the time to thick around apparently obvious truth until it didn't sound obvious anymore. Though, saying that, at other times I also wanted to land, to write something with a quickness, an economy, and a sense of an ending. Pace played a crucial role in all of this. But a lot happened in the last material edit. It was really a big question: how long could I leave it before I returned to a character or a question, how far apart could I space things before frustrating the reader – her patience, her memory?

PB:
The thing that occurred to me when thinking about 'form' was this idea of a *canon*. The fact that the book felt not exactly anti-canonical but rather a journey through your descriptions. You said on the way here that the sentences in the book "wobbled", which really resonates with me as a writer. I think about that wobble... I felt I could inhabit that space. I generally have a problem with writing that feels too definite, too shut down, and I felt that in that wobble – those contradictions – there is a constant opening out.

KB:
The project of the book, or the hope, was just to invite one person – one reader at a time – to think with me. I wanted to make a space where you would not necessarily agree with me, but you would feel enabled to think with me... and maybe be caught in the

white space and leave the question over time and return to it to see how you feel about it now. Perhaps this is obvious, but the book is very influenced by Barthes and his manner of thinking and writing. I did want to extend, in my own way, something of what he was doing in his lectures, which were speculative, and vulnerable, and open to and actively responsive to the audience. I don't mind wobbling, or my conclusions feeling provisional. I was trying to make a space where the complexities and all the nuances of this practice could finally appear. Not in the name of definitiveness, or taking a position once and for all. I don't intend to stop thinking about the questions translating brings me up against. But when it comes to definiteness in writing, the thing is: we do actually have a whole range of choices, or rhetorical moves, that we can make when we write something. The problem is that some tend to be valued more than others. Some tend to be associated with certain kinds of qualities more than others. We associate definiteness and certainty with authority – but why? I can't tell you how many times my work has been called 'whimsical' – as if, because it moves, or imagines, or goes dancing, it's somehow not serious.

LV:
The way you talk about it, you really feel this affective approach, even with your body.

KB:
We have this vast array of choices, of manners in writing, and my manner with this book was: "come with me and stay with me". That was the mode – or, again, the hope.

FP:
I was wondering, maybe you could tell us a bit about the story of Helen Lowe-Porter, what's happening in the book with her? And

linked to this, there is a point around page 90 where you describe your starting point in terms of translation through the criticism of Lowe-Porter. Can you say more?

KB:
Helen Lowe-Porter translated Thomas Mann into English, and she spent thirty-four years of her life devoted to the task of translating Thomas Mann intensively. Her translations were hugely successful and he became celebrated in America in particular. Having read her translation of *The Magic Mountain*, I became more curious about her as a translator. I discovered how, in the scholarly community of translation studies and especially Thomas Mann specialists, her work had been very deeply criticised in the early to mid-nineties. There was one article in particular which was published in the Times Literary Supplement just listing mistake after mistake. And yes, there are a lot of mistakes in her translation, apparently. This is the thing: as someone who can't read German, I wouldn't know. But the attack on her generated a small flurry of exchanges of letters to the Editor, and they brought up a lot of questions about the translator's responsibility, questions of expertise and qualifications. There was a lot of *Who did she think she was?* A lot of *amateur translator.* This idea that she had overestimated her own skills and capabilities. This fascinated and also baffled me: because isn't all translation practice, to some extent, about overestimating your own capabilities? I mean, how else could we authorise ourselves to even begin? All this made me curious to find out how she herself was thinking about her position, her practice. I found her correspondence fascinating and it feeds into the book. She is the one who, although she spent a great portion of her life translating Thomas Mann, calls translation 'a little art'. My aim was not to spin Helen Lowe-Porter as a heroine, exactly, but at least to take her seriously. To try and think with her for a while.

FP:

I guess what links all this together is the idea of collectivity. You connect, quite straightforwardly, the activity of translation with the idea of a collective project. From here you talk about translating as a sort of never-ending endeavour, and you talk about the importance of taking risks within such an endeavour. This whole process of continuity can be linked back to Lowe-Porter's story, while the process of collectivity could be brought back to Barthes, who was translated into different languages before. I guess what I am saying is that, by translating Barthes, you enter a community of previous translators... and as such you are also entering an ongoing discourse. I wanted to ask you specifically about the relationship between translating and this collective and continuous effort.

KB:

That's really interesting. I was in touch with another translator just recently who asked me about my experience of being in touch with other translators whilst I was translating, and actually I wasn't. But that was kind of my own fault, really. And it was because of anxiety – worried that my work was not good enough. Now I would be in touch with any translator, but at the time it was a very weirdly solitary job and I did feel very distanced from anything like a translation community. That said, I did have one very sustained and meaningful – and incredibly helpful – conversation with a Barthes specialist, a woman called Diana Knight, who was the appointed second reader for the manuscript. And although I mention solitude, it also wasn't solitary in the sense that translation is not solitary. As you say, to be a translator already means working with others, even if they are not present, or not even alive in the usual sense. It's a practice that is founded on being very close with at least one other.

Female Voice:
Did you have to spend a lot of time studying Barthes' personal life? To translate a piece of writing, do you need to know about the writer as an individual? And how would you do that? Do you have to research their personal life?

KB:
The materials that I was translating were quite particular because they were lecture notes, which were almost like a score. They were performed live in the Collège de France, so they weren't books. They were never intended to be books. They were notes with a view to being spoken aloud: they stop and start; they are often not full sentences. So, what I did do was listen to the recordings of the lectures so I could hear the voice. But interestingly, for a lecture course, Barthes was basing it in so much personal circumstance anyway. I mean, he is very clear that his project to write a novel follows a recent bereavement, the death of his mother. I was saying earlier that we have an array of rhetorical moves available to us, and some are more dominant or more accepted in some fields than others. You know, the sense that this is how to sound authoritative, this is how you talk about ideas, how you do criticism, how you do philosophy, how you do good intellectual work. And what I found deeply inspiring about the courses was how Barthes starts by saying: I will not repress the subject that I am. This is where I am speaking from. So, to answer your question, in Barthes's case the work was already so deeply and even I would say so strategically personal. He was deliberately collapsing the distinctions between philosophy, writing and life.

HENRY ANDERSEN:
One thing I also found interesting is that the book seems to try to hold two positions that seem contrary at the same time. And I

remember talking to a friend recently about how to try to have all these simultaneous possible meanings, and how by having to choose one you lose the others. I think this provisional element is very strong in the book and I'm curious if this is a way of dealing with loss.

KB:

One question I was constantly asking myself was how to affirm provisionality in such a way that is not uncommitted. Maybe there could be such a thing as a committed provisionality? It's like deciding if Lowe-Porter is a good translator or a bad translator, you know? I think it's complicated, and I think it's both. And I feel it should be possible to hold those two positions together in such a way that it doesn't feel like this this is a weak claim. But it's very interesting the way you relate that to the decisions you have to make: yes. Having at some point, to retain something, to set one option down, which means letting go, closing down or cancelling the other... in translation you can't have everything, you can't hold onto every possible translation solution, so you do have to choose, and then take responsibility for your choices. But even that is still temporary – somewhat temporary. Barthes has this amazing image of his mother's woollen stockings. When she would get a hole in them, she would stop the hole from laddering by putting a thumb in her mouth and stopping it with her saliva. He would say this is like writing: at a certain point in the endless play of meanings and possibilities, something gets set down. And you get this provisional immobilisation, this stopping of the now, which seems to be real. We are here now, in this provisional lovely space and it will last for a bit longer and then we disperse again.

Daniela Cascella
Voices, Subjects, Chimeras

1. Voices, Chimeras

It was written that tone is not the voice of the writer, but the intimacy of the silence the writer imposes on her speech. Writing in English I struggle to hear my voice, so I search for my tone in silenced words: I read, write. The silence I impose on my speech to hear its tone is magnified, deepened. How loud the echo, in the vast hall of deepened silence. I can nearly sense, together, the asphyxia and the echo, the smothering and the voicing; begin to make sense and not quite so.

It was also written that I do not speak with my voice, I speak with my voices. In English my voices are faint—faint for their not being clear and transparent, for their substance and subjects at times baffling, at times out of synch, full of histories and literatures so obscure or specific that they might sound empty in the ears of many. Who will receive? Who will tune in? When you are outside certain legitimate circles of cultural anything, who is there, who is willing to hear? Most crucially: is amplification necessary, when certain signals demand to stay faint? Caught between the necessity of transmitting faint sounds, and the high possibility of not being received, I long for a type of hearing—that is reading, that is writing—attuned to detect other faint voices, those that won't ever become loud enough because if they do, they get distorted and lose texture. Better to tune in the hearing, than to force a faint signal to scream. These faint signals may appear isolated because of the non immediacy of references or the cultural context they hold. And yet they stay, hover, like the impressions left by the telling of a story, by the playing of a record.

The faint voices might sound as if they are speaking about nothing at all. But one can hear in them the density of a resonance closest to their material, the material of the apparent absence they echo, swarming with impossible conversations. Don Quijote said that to read a book in translation is like viewing a Flemish tapestry from the back. To write of subjects, cultures, words that are *not* translated is to convey a hallucination of the tapestry, a reverie encountered in a void space resounding with faint voices.

This silence of mine when writing in English will never be entirely mine, and I can only perceive and finally hear *mine* as a storehouse to extract from. A strong sense of artifice is at play: not having one voice means having to construct it, in a heightened awareness toward the workings of rhetoric, toward writing as assembling, words found and connected by kinship. These voices are mine and the mine is deep, some of it unmapped, some of it dark, some of it with precious stones, some of it with dull rock and moss and useless damp surfaces.

I long for a form of critical writing that inhabits, is haunted by, and echoes in the silent mines of its subjects: literature, sounds, fictions of the self. I call it *chimeric* writing. It is implausible, and it exists the moment it is named, the moment it is written: a monstrous creature made up of different parts that move together. Shaped by its subjects through inhabitation, echo, and sympathy, chimeric writing tunes into each voice, flawed and necessary as any voice is; with fleeting moments of harmony, and the inevitable fractures of interference and noise. Sometimes the signal is heavily distorted, sometimes it is perceived as noise, sometimes it is faint, or loud and clear, sometimes frequencies interfere, sometimes they beat. It silences the voices not quite all mine, and transforms them into its tone, its true form an image of echo and chimera

e ti chiamo ti chiamo chimera, chimera chimes, la mia forma vera, un'imagine d'Eco e di Chimera.

2. Subjects: The Rule Of The Game, The Rule Of The I

The realisation that I could be many voices—that self-in-language is groundless but not without grounds, and takes form in a malleable realm of something more and something else than words where I could be beyond my self—came to me at an early age, at the time when I learned to read and write. Learning the alphabet, learning to put together words on a page as fixed signs, happened in the same span of months when I became aware of a different accent: not the vowels of my parents, the clipped and closed *e*'s of Southern Italy, but the more open, rounded sounds of the region around Rome. When spoken out loud, my first name was in fact two names: Daniéla, Danièla. There I was, groundless but not without grounds, hearing my two selves, marvelling at what words could do and be as they were pronounced and transformed, rather than what they were, in fixity. The revelation that the same name could sound in two different ways, at home and at school—*at least* in two different ways, and who knew how many more—was not perceived as a crisis, but as a spur for understanding the transformative drive of sound, the mobility I could find while reaching out through listening, outside of my 'self': Daniéla, Danièla. I could be a trickster, at times I could hide, or I could be many people. Michel Leiris reports a similar experience at the beginning of his autobiography. He's a child, and has just been told that he's pronounced a word in the wrong way. For the first time he becomes aware of 'language, whose life outside me, filled with strangeness, I had been allowed to glimpse... I was dazed, seized by a sort of vertigo. Because this word, which I had said incorrectly and had just discovered was not really what I had thought it was before then, enabled me to sense obscurely—through the sort of deviation or displacement it impressed on my mind—how articulated language, the arachnean tissue of my relations with others, went beyond me, thrusting its mysterious antennae in all directions.' Leiris's autobiography is entitled *La règle du jeu*—'jeu', 'game', is also heard as 'je', 'I': the rule of the game is also the rule of the I, autobiography is not tied to claims of authenticity but it is, from the outset, a game, its rules laid out through the sliding, ambiguous, arachnean tissue of sound. Who's the I here? JeuJe, Igame, the trickster, the many-voiced, many voices spinning on and around the singular, like someone once said: groundless, but not without grounds.

Echoes, Mines, Chimeras

Alejandra Pizarnik, 'Cornerstone', *Extracting The Stone Of Madness: Poems 1962-72,* tr. Yvette Siegert, New York: New Directions, 2016
Amelia Rosselli, *La libellula*, Milano: SE, 1996
Dino Campana, 'La Chimera', *Canti Orfici*, Milano: Rizzoli, 1989
Cristina Campo, *Gli imperdonabili*, Milano: Adelphi, 1987; *Sotto falso nome*, Milano: Adelphi, 1998
Elfriede Jelinek, Nobel Prize Speech, 2004
Gaspara Stampa, rima CXXIV, *Rime,* Milano: Rizzoli, 1994
Giorgio Manganelli, *Le interviste impossibili*, Milano: Adelphi, 1997
Maurice Blanchot, 'The Essential Solitude', *The Gaze Of Orpheus And Other Literary Essays,* tr. Lydia Davis, Barrytown: Station Hill, 1981
Michel Leiris, *Scratches*, tr. Lydia Davis, Baltimore and London: The Johns Hopkins University Press, 1997
Robert Duncan, *The H.D. Book,* Berkeley, Los Angeles, London: The University of California Press, 2011
Roberto Calasso, *La rovina di Kasch,* Milano: Adelphi, 1983
The voice of Carmelo Bene
The collected silences of D.C.

Nadia Hebson
I See You

You are offering me an atmosphere of thinking. Exact conditions, circumstances evaporate when I close the book, my empty headedness in the form of recountable details, names, facts, all absent, now only a marginal embarrassment aged 45 because this, your elastic gesture of paying close attention, is intensely familiar. A form of thinking, reflection, happening several layers further down. As in actually down inside me. And in its very existence a kicking against, an abandoning, a dismissal of the constraints, prejudices, internalised notions of something approaching control grounded in the conventions of thinking (patriarchal) as I would name it. And now there emerges something as solid as a critique of truth and objectivity through something as quivering, fragile, responsive, expansive as a series of resonances, ambivalences, loves, scepticisms, intuitions, commitments, hunches, misunderstandings, admirations and hard thoughts. Through extended, keen attention. In this very moment, between these very people. To pit these elements against one another is to miss the point, but damn it between the factual and the fictive, the private and the public, the objective and the subjective, a revision of all kinds is being set in motion.

When and where is the work happening? And mimicry?

Do I read through some fractious anxiety? I have long ago learnt to override such potential debilitations, so, anxiety as a productive force then, hyper vigilance, ultra- attentiveness, a shrewd deployment of qualities for me insinuated by the conditions of my gender.

I will not (can't and won't) speak with a faux cadence, a modulated pitch in an attempt to mimic an acceptable confidence. That is another kind of mimicry, one assumed in bad faith. But this is what this actually sounds like, this is what this actually looks like, how to find a way of working that approximates these realities, these attentions, these gentle and tacit refusals and direct choices, confident. Provisionality. Veracity.

There is another kind of mimicry. Informed by watchfulness, attention, empathy and imagination. Performed in good faith through sheer necessity. Must it be politically and ethically stated? In a plain and clear (plangent?) voice? I cannot leave it to the vagaries of chance or the hopes of *subtlety* appealing to the attentive mind, this *good* work. In the future I would spot myself and start a conversation, my dress a request to converse. But I am not seen and must extend the invitation or at least state the terms of the engagement, with some implied force.

(as I need to converse with friends).

Did persistent self-scrutiny, self-censoring, a heightened self-awareness set this attention in motion? A negative interiority turned inward to then be turned outward again. Frustration and then, thank god, creative friendship enabling a volte-face. Is it misplaced to understand these sensitivities as originating in a female experience, conditioning? I do not claim the experience exclusively but cannot not mention these vital circumstances.

And mimicry?

Sometimes I read to find a mirror, to reflect myself back to myself. A way to make oneself visible, seen in the brilliance of others, heard in the world. I freely admit it contains a self-regard but to seek allies, even in misunderstanding can shore oneself up. *She cannot work without some semblance of self-regard.* As a private activity, it is difficult to put this in the service of unrestrained thinking. To clarify, this reading serves not as an example, this reading is a call and response, wilfully open. Originating in imagined shared concerns. Tripping up on unexpected suggestions, critical extensions, gentle provocations. The hope is an echo heard returned in amity, but in moments of doubt it may represent an overwriting or an annotation written bluntly in pen.

I am a painter who rarely paints and I endlessly look for the book about painting that I want to read.

Incrementally *translating* the work of Christina Ramberg for these last nine years. And she herself an artist who attentively *translates* those subtle, wordless conversations conducted between women, through the medium of dress, alongside other private gestures that simply connect an interiority, a psychological complexity with a hardened public projection. The sheerness of a fabric, the particularities of a cuff sleeve, the pairing of a 70's leather skirt with a 30's silk slip. Painting, like wearing clothing, where the conditions of the medium, it's established meanings, are rewritten to suggest other ways of being. Confounding. The act of dressing, a productive confusion that shortcuts gender binaries and the strictures of class - these the familiar inequalities and other enduring exclusions. A refusal to enact established assumptions and unquestioned conditions that continue to unnerve.

Her painting travelling faster than her own thinking and my work, my *translation* seemingly so slight it is rarely perceived.

I am a painter that rarely paints in the ways you have imagined. But these works: her paintings, your writing, my painting, are an invitation to attend, to closely consider these strange resonances and their inexhaustive possibilities. In form, in being a truer *truth,* in the willingness to change direction. A commanding and solid voice disregarded for something that contains the directions of thought.

'Artists for re-creation monitor present day comprehension through new iterations. Things don't mean the same thing forever. Most things disappear.'

Lynne Tillman, *The Translation Artist*

Paul Becker
Somewhere in Sontag

I thought I had read it somewhere in Sontag. I thought it was in her introduction to *The Walk.* Of course when I went back to it, it was no longer there (which isn't to say that it never existed…) It was a long sentence, or so I imagined, a statement about what she loved best about the novel, about what possibilities were or could be contained within it and how, for her, the novel should try not only to be the ultimate experimental form but should also attempt to incorporate the world entire, all of it, as well as all of Literature, each and every genre, humour, horror, poetics, theoretics with wildly colliding styles, contrapuntal languages, the shift and drag of tangent, backwater, discourse, argument, contradiction. Her novel should allow the pornographic and the mathematic to partake of the same page. The epic encompassed within the miniature, *Nouveau Roman* colliding with historical fiction or *bildungsroman.* Each such novel, an unprecedented event in and of itself, and like Joyce's *Ulysses* or Kavan's *Ice,* each forming and simultaneously surmounting its own individual canon.

I admit to a slight contradiction in being both sneeringly suspicious of famous writers telling me how to write and at the same time, an avid, in fact *desperate* reader of any such golden rules. Later, I also convinced myself Hilary Mantel had said something about taking everything you've ever written and putting it all into one big, sprawling, madcap work and letting it find its own form.

Both the fantasised Mantel and the imagined Sontag dictums only go to prove to me the writer I am not. I am plainly seeking some kind of endorsement for knowing nothing about what I am doing. My inability to structure, to craft, to hone a text is excused by the one, my lack of empathy for the reader as well as any sense of stylistic or narrative consistency, absolved by the other. Isaac Babel staked a claim for the importance of 'the right to write badly' and perhaps there really could be a place for ambitious failure in writing, for not being completely sure, for not knowing. I admit I arrived here as a reader only, purely as a punter and although this ostensibly places me in no worse position than those who have put the weird hours into acquiring the requisite nuts and bolts for fiction, I still have a secret need to be told I am going about it all the wrong way, that there is a hidden doorway, a formal shortcut.

In terms of painting, there is also an understandable focus in the minds of many tyro artists and their teachers that the acquisition of 'skills' is the shortest path to enlightenment. For some, who knows, maybe it is? For me, 'not knowing' doesn't equate to some blissful prelapsarian state before the word art even existed. Art is traduced enough as a preserve of 'intellectuals' as it is (intellectual being still, so sadly, a pejorative term) traduced, far too often, by artists themselves. In fact things are more complicated and not knowing is a profound *embracing*, not an abandoning of art making and of thinking. Perhaps skills had better be attempted, even coopted but I don't believe they are to be relied upon. Yes, this is a more dubious path. In painting, works that evidence craft and technical accomplishment are more readily praised and content, subject are much tougher to talk about than the dread, unassailable fortress of *process.* Painters, like printmakers are not always at their most penetrating when they speak to us of *how* things are made; the *why* is discussed surprisingly little, even in art schools. But we are not technicians and those seeking virtuoso skillsets *only,* have no further to look than the nearest youtube tutorial.

Not knowing, in this sense, means not being able to position oneself above the reader or the viewer. That means you/we also, to some extent, share a space in the dark. If neither of us fully know, fully understand, can fully gauge any available meaning then suddenly the space between reach and grasp becomes available. In that nuanced space, the work exists, it breathes. In that space, the autonomy of the work is engendered and afforded, as is, potentially, our desire to participate, to activate, to inhabit. It could be the issue is allowing oneself to allow for that space, to allow for question, for doubt, critique, for thinking, for dreaming, for breathing. There is a certain autonomy at least when things are good, and a certain fluidity in the exchange between the viewer and the viewed.

That writing or visual art are containers of emotion is a standard definition. I would go further. The most interesting and elusive work is not an empty vessel, a tabula rasa. No, because of that space I mentioned, I believe such work contains emotion as much as it contains autonomous thought and if we accept that as a fundamental, I would also posit the notion that an autonomous vessel containing both emotion (feeling) and intellect (thinking) can make a claim to a unique form of sentience. I think some texts, some artworks, really are alive, obviously not as we understand life but they do have a singular existence, a state of being involving time and space and dream. I think books, paintings, rest there on their shelves, on their walls but they are not inanimate, they hum and fizz and bristle with life even when they are not being read or observed.

I believe there is a similar sentient translation and exchange when we look into the eye of a wonderful text or a mysterious painting as when we catch the glance of a horse or a smiling dog, but that's another story.

A Table Made Again for the First Time - a collective discussion with Kate Briggs

Bureau des Réalités, Bruxelles
September 2018

PART 2

NADIA HEBSON:

Can the provisionality be seen as gendered? The translation being able to puncture the authority of the author? We have these examples of women who were supposedly amateurs and they dared to go against this oppression. I took that almost as a feminist gesture and got really kind of heartened by it. Is there an argument that this is deflating some sort of patriarchal authoritarian, wholly objective, academic way of constituting the practice? Sometimes I think it's useful to see it in these terms: to make a provisional claim that this might be an alternative way to understand things.

KB:

Yes, I think so absolutely. Though it has taken me a long time to get to thinking this. I said something earlier about feeling the book was somehow in keeping with Barthes's own project in his lecture courses, or at least in keeping with his manner of asking questions, circulating ideas, bringing practices of thinking and art-making into conversation with the details of everyday life. Something he says in his lectures which has stuck with me is that they are all about changing the rhetorical conditions of the intellectual, which I took him to mean something like: Where do we tend to locate the emergence of serious ideas? What kind of voice do you hear as authoritative? What kind of manner? Coming from what kind of body? And situated in what kinds of spaces? I see this changing or varying or opening of the rhetorical conditions – basically how to speak and what to speak of – as a feminist project – though I don't find the tools for that in Barthes. Or I don't find them offered out to me – I guess I've had to claim them. The right to write about the scenes of my life as scenes of thinking. The right to productive uncertainty. Also the projects of decolonising, de-centering, multiplying languages and perspectives. But all of that said, I would be careful of provisionality for the sake of provisionality. This comes back to the gesture, the risky, bold, sometimes violent, sometimes authoritarian, will-to-certainty gesture of setting something down. Translators do this too – they have to. It is part of their work; it is the task they, we, take on. But then again – thinking out loud – I think I would also say that all this, like so much of social life, comes down to manners: to how we speak to each other, how we listen to each other or fail to, how we create spaces with our books and bodies and works – in your case your paintings and installations – for others, or fail to. There again is a set of decisions to be made. I recognise that I do have a certain degree of agency – I can to some degree choose how I speak, how I engage with other people and their work and ideas, what forms of address, what tones I use. And generally speaking I want to do this with curiosity and thoughtfulness and, I don't know, warmth – why not? I write at length in the book about 'tact' – a form of being responsive, and adjusting your behaviour in relation to other. These qualities are not without power, they have the force of attentiveness, they make things happen in the world, the absence of them can make things not happen. They often get reduced – you know, but I don't think they should be reduced too quickly...

FP:
I would like to ask you if you want to read page 115. So just to put this into context: we are here in full discussion around Barthes, and the main question is: 'Why write?' And then, throughout the next five pages, the reasoning feels like a sort of cascade: 'Why write' becomes also 'Why read', which becomes desire, which becomes expectations etc. etc.

KB:
I will read the page then:
The desire to write comes (is the feeling you get from) certain readings:

the kind of reading that agitates you into making a trace of itself. Or to put it another way, and reaching a little further for an answer to his outrageous, unanswerable question [because on the previous page I had quoted Barthes asking 'Why Writing?' Why, out of all of life's activities, why do writing more than anything else?] *Barthes arrives at the following claim: 'to want to write is to want to re-write', he says. And then: 'Every beautiful work, or even every work to make an impression, every impressive work functions as a desired work, but I would say, and it's here that it starts to get interesting, that every work I read as desirable, even as I'm desiring it, I experience it as incomplete and somehow lost because I didn't do it myself, and I have to in some way retrieve it by re-doing it; in this way, to write is to want to rewrite: I want to add myself actively to that which is beautiful and that lack, as we might put it with an old verb: that I require'.*[1]

FP:
This was a page that some of the invited artists and writers chose and wanted to discuss today. Paul Becker was one of them, who interestingly enough, apart from being a writer, is also a painter.

PB:
This section and especially this page is related to something strange that happened to me. There was a kind of dropping-out that sometimes happens when a particular text or a particular line really resonates. I find it really difficult to talk about it, but it felt very important to me as a painter because it felt like you were talking about a kind of opening-out that happens in this idea of writing, of rewriting. For me, when looking at a painting, when the painting works in the same way as this text works, one undergoes a very particular feeling of desire which offers the potential for one's own feelings to form

1. Kate Briggs, *This Little Art*, p. 115, Fitzcarraldo Editions, London 2017

part of it, in a sense *rewriting* it. 'The kind of reading that agitates you into making a trace of itself…' Barthes is describing that wanting to write is wanting to re-write, to 'add himself actively to that which is beautiful.' Maybe it does work, but for me there is a real connection with trying to figure out whether it's possible to extrapolate from these descriptions that certain texts, and certain paintings as well, have an autonomy, yes, but also actively encourage a space for that adding of oneself, and that desire. As a painter I often talk about images having a 'life', images being autonomous, about 'killing' a painting by overworking it, and I'm interested in the same thing happening here: a residual quality that remains in texts or in paintings that allows for that issuing in of desire.

KB:
Actively encouraging a space for that adding of oneself – which is a form of desire. Yes! That's beautiful and I think you're right. Some works do this, some works make a space, a welcome or a kind of inn for the desires of others, and some don't. And maybe you can only ever really be sure when you've failed to do this – killing it – than you ever can of having achieved it.

FEMALE VOICE:
I was also touched by this. I'm not an artist, but this is quite universal and inspiring for every sort of creativity. Everybody can relate to this kind of feeling, of seeing something that they loved so much, and wishing they had done it. And I think this kind of relationship, this love and affective relationship that Barthes explains through reading and writing is so pure in everything regarding creativity. Creativity is always linked to this notion of desire. You can't do anything if you don't have this desire, this sort of erotic approach for what has been done and that you want, maybe, to transcend.

KB:

But I think what it is also very explicitly about here, is being-in-relation-to, or maybe even being indebted-to. Like, my work cannot exist without the work, and therefore the labour of others. What I find so interesting – but I think others can find so provocative – about the translator's position is that it is clear and unapologetic. The translator's writing would not exist without support. You know, clearly. Likewise, in his project of novel writing, which would have involved making something new, Barthes sets down his tutor texts from the beginning, he is saying very clearly that whatever will be written will be in response, indirectly, a mediated response, to existing work, written by other people. What would happen, I wonder, if we were all a bit more easy and willing to recognise this - how our work depends on others? Having approached writing under my name by way of translation I think, I hope, I'll always be ready to acknowledge this, but I don't think that's a necessarily generalised position. I don't know, what do you think?

FEMALE VOICE:

It's interesting. What I think about is wanting to make things that you can't find, or like you said earlier, trying to find yourself in works and not finding yourself there, so having to make that thing happen. That's how I see it mostly in terms of looking at others and responding.

FEMALE VOICE:

Isn't this something about stewarding yourself in order to do something. I think in contemporary living there is an enclosed proximity or thinking through someone else's work. And that love and close attention, and thinking through their practice can generate the urgency to make your own. It's an acknowledgment of that intimacy. You might be looking at these other works, working through them because you can't find exactly what you are looking for. I'm interested in how historically those associations might have occurred, and how originality came into play. *This Little Art* seems to be another way of making work.

KB:
Yes, I think I see... forms of closeness that are not about reproduction or translation or making again but about finding what the works themselves didn't even know they could offer. This comes back to what Paul was saying, doesn't it? There has to be something singular about this encounter, for each of us. I mean, we don't all find the same things, or feel the same way about the same books or artworks, they don't all open a space for all of us, create an urgency to do likewise...

FP:
I thought there is something about the body - of the translator, the book - a physicality about your approach to reading and writing. When you stood up, stood up to read, we felt this physical reaction. Another page of your book that was pointed out was page 119. I don't know if I completely understood...

KB:
Should we go to that page?

FP:
Yes, please. Page 119. We can read it...

KB:
Just to situate this in relation to the last passage, Barthes has just claimed that: 'writing comes from reading, and to want to write is to want to re-write,' and he offers various forms that this can

take, and one of them is copying, just copying something out. In the lecture courses, he has a list of further forms, but this is my intervention, I guess, because what he doesn't say – the practice he doesn't think to mention – is translation.

Translation doesn't appear on Barthes list. But I hear this talk of the desire to write as the desire for the focused ambition to write the thing itself, only this time by myself, as one possible version – as a very precise way of rephrasing my own experience – of the impulse to translate. Translation conceived as a means of writing the other's work out with your own hands in your own setting, your own time and in your own language, with all the attention, thinking and searching, the testing and invention that the task requires. Translation as a laborious way of making the work present to yourself, the finding it again yourself, for yourself. Translation as a responsive and appropriative practising *at the level of the sentence, working it out, a* work-out *on the basis of the desired work whose energy source is the inclusion of the new and different vitality that comes with and from me.*[2]

NATASHA SOOBRAMANIEN:

This is such a generative work. For some reason when I read it, I was thinking about how it articulated something for me about why I found it difficult to read the translated work of a female writer... for instance of Elfriede Jelinek[3], whose translations were done by a man. I was resistant to this idea of reading the translation by a man. I don't know if this is something that means anything to anyone here, but after reading your book, I feel more alive to the idea of

---

2. Kate Briggs, *This Little Art*, p. 119, Fitzcarraldo Editions, London 2017
3. Elfriede Jelinek (b. 1946) is an Austrian novelist. She was awarded the Nobel Prize for Literature in 2004. Most of her novels have been translated into English by Chalmers.

the body of the translator in the translated work. My first novel[4] was translated by Nathacha Appanah, a woman of an origin that is deeply involved in the book, so I felt very happy that she was working on it, because it felt really right to have her re-write the book.

KB:
Yes, who does the translations – and how this matters. I completely agree. But on the other hand, I also find it difficult. I mean: this question of who is the right translator, who is the appropriate translator, what do they look like. I guess in part because my published translations have been of work done by men of a different generation, of a different moment. There is nothing that marks me out as being a particularly qualified or appropriate translator of Roland Barthes. I think that's stated quite clearly in the book, the contingency of it, of how it came to be me. The me who was then moved by the work, who became attached to it – or attached myself to it. I think I would want to hold on to the thought that this is also what reading does, or can do: it allows for improbable, unlikely, ungrounded identification and feelings and attachments to other kinds of bodies. This has to be the case. I mean, it would awful if it weren't. Reading offers the possibility of at least provisionally collapsing those positions and identities that hold us.

NATASHA SOOBRAMANIEN:
I think the female writer I'm talking about, well, her resistance felt so visceral and physical in the sense of difficulty, that I couldn't get over that a man had translated her work.

---

4. Natasha Soobramanien, *Genie and Paul*, Myriad Editions, 2012. The French edition was translated by Nathacha Appanah and published by Gallimard in 2018.

KB:

I agree that this must be a question a translator asks themselves when taking on a project: am I the right person to do this? Especially if they already have some power, some choice in the matter. Could I not step aside for someone else, for this? Yet, depending on the context, I would also want to hold out for the unlikely match, as long as it doesn't only work in the powerful white translator's favour: the chance of the more improbable, unexpected pairing...

FEMALE VOICE:

To further this idea of pairings, I'm also interested in the idea of collaborative translations, because I wasn't aware of it, and I really didn't think about it until I went to a presentation of Chris Kraus's book in Brussels and there was a picture of the translation into Dutch, and it was done by two people. I wondered if you ever translated in collaboration?

KB:

Yes, I did in my first translation, an early text by Michel Foucault, his thesis on Kant. I did it with my friend Roberto Nigro, who is Italian, and he was worried about his writing capacity in English. So, the idea initially was that he would read Foucault, understand it and translate it into his English, while I would then revise the whole thing. But we soon realised that this was not going to work, because in order to go back to the French and find an English word that worked, well, I too needed to understand it. But I think in the end this process gave me the confidence to pitch translation projects on my own...

FP:

I'm fascinated by all this because one of the elements I wanted to talk to you about is this idea of symmetry. You obviously realise there are three women who are translating the work of three very well-known men. I notice it, and you talked about this symmetry, of a powerful cultural figure that is translated by their opposite gender etc. So, I wanted to ask about the fact that you didn't meet Barthes. Because the other two women had a direct relationship with the two male writers while you didn't.

KB:
Maybe I would wonder about symmetry, which suggests balance, or something like an even distribution of power. I think in all three cases this distribution was clearly uneven. These three very prominent, respected, canonised men. But at the same time, and this is where I would want both answers, in holding the contradictory positions together, it is important to recognise that the translator – although still a generally undervalued contributor to culture, politics, art, life – is intensely powerful. Her decisions are her decisions, and they stand, they direct readings, actually for a long time, sometimes for generations, until there is interest or the possibility of doing the translation again. It's true that I didn't have a direct relationship with Barthes. I didn't know him. I met him in his writings, and in the recordings of his lectures. I went and stood once, in the street where he lived. This comes back, maybe, to what I was trying to say in response to Natasha's question. I believe in books as meeting places; I really do. I love the way they open. I love that they are cheap, relatively speaking. I love how they offer a means of bringing someone else's energy into my own home, and into interaction with my own private, everyday life. So I would say I didn't know Barthes directly but I have met him and I expect keep meeting him, regularly, over my life-time.

PB:
What's the next thing that you will be working on?

KB:

Well, I'm working on a book. After saying all that, it would have to be a book. When I describe *This Little Art,* I say it's like an essay trying to be a novel, but I think this next thing is more obviously like a novel in the sense that it has characters and it's not in the first person. It's in the third person, but it is still committed to the essayistic, and the more explicit exploration of ideas. I think it's about staying with certain things – people, especially very young people, a baby, questions – over time.

Alejandro Zambra
Translating a Person (I)

I

The gringo was twelve years old, like nearly all of us, and his name was Michael González or John Pérez or something like that: a common English first name and a last name that was equally common in Spanish. He had grown up in Chicago with Chilean parents, so his Spanish was almost the same as ours and his English sounded like the movies. Fascinated, we'd ask him to speak it for us at recess, and the gringo was shy but also happy and patient, so he'd play along. Like a magician revealing his simplest tricks, he'd ramble on in a hushed voice about any old subject, and he even answered our questions, which were all very basic: how do you say *pico?* (dick); how do you say *zorra?* (pussy); how do you say *culiar?* (fuck).

One day, after a group presentation, the English teacher decided that Michael's (or John's) pronunciation was deficient, and she gave him a 5 out of seven. It took us a minute to realise the teacher didn't even know the gringo was a gringo. She was a thirty-something woman with a chubby face and cheerful demeanor, her eyebrows smeared with blue eyeshadow, always just about to smile or smoke. We loved her, she was nice, much warmer and more approachable than most of our teachers. That afternoon we tried, among several of us, to explain her mistake. She wanted proof, but the gringo was feeling especially shy, hiding away behind his notebooks. Finally, when the silence was becoming unbearable, he stood up and launched into a surprisingly loquacious soliloquy, much louder and faster that he tended to speak at recess, his face bright red as if speaking English were something to be ashamed of, and there was also something desperate in his incomprehensible— to us—torrent of words. He spoke for about five minutes, and I didn't understand anything except for the word *Chile*, which made an appearance every so often. "I didn't know you were a gringo," was all the teacher said, in an effort to hide her humiliation.

The episode now strikes me as essentially comic, but at the time it seemed tragic and we tried to file it away immediately, because the teacher's sudden seriousness represented a threat. We preferred her—needed her—to be happy: it was much more important that she return our love than that we learned English.

From music or movies or just from the ambient noise, I had or thought I had a certain precarious familiarity with the English language. I was excited about studying it, and although there are so many things about that time that I have forgotten or twisted, I have a clear memory of the pleasure—the pride—that came from stringing together a sentence and achieving the miracle of communicating in another language. One afternoon however, I raised my hand automatically mid-question, with only a vague idea of what was being asked. I found myself facing a dead end, and I tried to find a way out by uttering the word *alimentation*—I had the paradigm in my head of words like *pronunciation*, *information*, or *generation*, and I steeled myself to run the risk. The results were disastrous, because the teacher let out one of her contagious guffaws, then said, calmly and sweetly: that word doesn't exist.

There was a painful outburst of shouts and laughter, and I immediately imposed upon myself the quite reasonable punishment that I would never participate in that class again for the rest of the year. I also decided to keep my distance from the gringo, who had no skin in that game but was still the official representative of that language in which I had failed miserably. Toward the end of the year we only said hi to each other, though with a friendly smile. One morning we ran into each other two blocks from school, and the prospect of walking together and being pretty much forced to talk was uncomfortable for both of us. But I think by that point my shyness was already false, so I set off talking about any old thing and he livened up, too. He told me he was leaving the school because his family had to go back to Chicago. I told him I would miss him, though I don't know if it was true, and he seemed happy I said it, but maybe he didn't care. I asked him what he thought now about the English teacher. He said he liked her. Just to throw fuel on the fire I asked him if she was, in his opinion, a good teacher. He said yes. I reminded him of the incident at the beginning of the year, and, imbued with an air of calm, in a tone somewhere between philosophical and melancholic, he said that there were many ways of speaking English. Then I reminded him of my own incident, also at the beginning of the year, but the gringo didn't remember it. I didn't believe him, I thought he was just saying it to be nice, but apparently he really didn't remember. Minutes before class started, when we were already seated in our opposite corners of the classroom, he came over to me to tell me that he was almost sure that the word *alimentation* did exist; that it was an old-fashioned word that wasn't used much, but it existed. That possibility had not even occurred to me. At recess we headed for the library and asked for a dictionary. "I'm almost sure that word exists," repeated the gringo in a nervous murmur while we furiously turned the pages. And there it was, we found it: I even think the word *alimentation* shone in that immense, old dictionary.

2

When I was fifteen, at a party, a group of blond boys from a bilingual school—in my memory they appear as caricatures of jock rich kids—started to speak in very loud English about their momentary enemies, who were us. We got the general idea—they accused us of being dark, of being ugly, of being hoodlums—but we didn't understand enough to answer them. I was impressed when I heard them speak so easily and it made me livid, of course, not to understand or to understand so little. After a few shoves we were kicked out of the party, and since we got back so early to the house where we were staying (Parraguez's house), no one was home, so we opened a few bottles of wine we found in the storage room. As we celebrated what must have been the first or second or at most the fifth time in our lives we'd been drunk, we thought it was funny to imitate those English-speaking, fancy-school boys, and that's how a longstanding and lamentable tradition got started: every time we got drunk we started to speak English, and we even used the expression "speak English" as a euphemism to allude to those drunken nights.

Some years later, in 1998, I applied for a job as an international phone operator and I claimed I spoke English at an intermediate level; my experience of speaking, though, was limited almost exclusively to those ludicrous conversations as the parties wrapped up. I didn't know English, but neither would it be precise to say I was ignorant of it. I had wanted to keep learning, but without *real* desire, because the idea of improving my English fought against the impression that it was more worthwhile to study tae kwon do or violin or palmistry or anything else, even any other language, because English was always there anyway. It was almost impossible not to absorb a few rudiments just from the atmosphere, and that, combined with the two class hours a week during six years of school, fostered my sense that I knew something, or that, in any case, it wasn't urgent to keep studying English. What's more, the constant lectures about the importance of English in today's competitive world took away my desire to learn. I wanted to learn English so I could read novels or watch movies without glasses or better pronounce lyrics by the Kinks or Neil Young, not so I could get ahead in business.

Luckily, the job wasn't difficult. I managed to communicate reasonably well with most of my colleagues scattered around the world, and I didn't even get nervous when I had to talk with my counterparts in Paris or Amsterdam or Tokyo, because we all spoke more or less the same bad English. But when I had to call the office in London or Chicago or Sydney it all turned into an uphill struggle, because then I had to speak, as we said, English-English. We personi-fied our communication problems in the figure of Chad, an arrogant phone operator in the Chicago office who missed no opportunity to manifest how awful he found our English or our service or our existence. "I had to talk to a Chad," or "I got a couple of Chads today" meant, specifically, that we had had an unpleasant and slightly humiliating conversation. In my case the Chad was almost always Chad himself (the original). "There are many different ways of speaking English," I remember telling him once, secretly proud of citing the gringo. Chad didn't reply.

Around that time, as a convoluted way of improving my English, I started translating poetry. It was just a way to quiet my own internal pangs at the boss's urging to improve our English. Now that I think about it, my immediate past held four semesters of Latin, which we learned by translating, so taking on English as if it were a dead language came more or less naturally. Sometimes I didn't even translate, anyway: what I did was just take notes that would allow me to read Auden or Emily Dickinson or Robert Creeley with greater depth. To read Ezra Pound's early poetry in English, for example, was to me as laborious as reading César Vallejo or Gabriela Mistral in Spanish. I'm not thinking only of the supposed difficulties, but also of the reader's frame of reference, the rhythm, the kind of concentration required. I tried to correct or adapt or "Chilean-ise" the very Spanish translations of Auden or Emily Dickinson put out by Barcelona publishers. As for Creeley, none of whose books existed in Spanish then, I merely tried for an initial reading.

Somewhere, I hope, there must still exist a red notebook, Torre brand, with my Spanish versions of Emily Dickinson. There were no more than fifteen poems, each one copied dozens of times, since I thought and still think that is the best way to translate: obstinately transcribe those numerous, nearly identical versions until one of them takes hold and prevails. Of the many translations of those poems I only remember my version of one of Dickinson's best-known poems, the one that begins: "I never hear the word "Escape"/Without a quicker blood/ A sudden expectation – / A flying attitude!". My translation takes the form of hendecasyllables, and somehow that makes me happy and ashamed at the same time. I feel like the poem is 'normalised,' naturalized, fenced in. I remember I wanted to translate 'a quicker blood' as "*el ritmo de mi sangre se acelera*," but then I lost the rhythm. I also remember how much I struggled with the first line of each quartet.

The habit of reading in English gradually extended from poetry to prose. I read stories and novels, but I cheated at first, because I was really rereading texts that I already knew and adored in Spanish translation, like *The Subterraneans*, one of Jack Kerouac's less celebrated novels, which to me is magnificent, in particular for its devastating ending.

I remember the trip from Puerto Montt to Parral in the slow, budget train, when I read a novel in English for the first time with no dictionary (I know it sounds like 'no hands'). The satisfaction that I *was reading quickly* arose every once in a while with all its distracting potential. The experience unleashed such joy in me that I didn't even have time to consider whether I liked the novel or not. I only thought about it a couple of days later. And no, I hadn't liked it, not at all: I'd confused understanding with enjoyment. I think it was a long time before I read a novel in English and managed a certain aesthetic emotion that was similar, or at least comparable, to what I would experience in Spanish.

3.

The same way that a movie filmed in Santiago always retains, for me, a certain documentary warmth, as if it weren't entirely a movie, a film set in New York always seems, from the start, *too much* like a movie. That's why, the first time I went to New York, I found it hard to take the city seriously. I was there to present two of my books that had been translated to English, but I had a little time to get used to the city first. Those were meandering days, effusive and unreal: I felt like an actor, or more like an extra; specifically, like one of those jackasses who as soon as they get the chance sneak a look at the camera.

The afternoon of the event, EJ van Lanen—a charming guy who at the time was my editor at Open Letter—came over to the corner where I, terrified, was smoking my pre-penultimate cigarette. He asked me, purely out of politeness, if I was nervous. I should have replied with a little laugh, even a cough would have sufficed, but I liked EJ so much and so wanted us to be friends that I tried to give a more elaborate answer. I flashed on Emily Dickinson and I told him: "Well, I feel like a quicker blood." EJ thought I was going to faint and offered to make arrangements to cancel the event and take me to the hospital. My intention was not, of course, to cite Emily Dickinson, I simply used the resources I had at hand. I was able to communicate and make friends (and to make a fool of myself, which has historically been, in my case, a pretty effective way to make friends), but in spite of the hours of—so to speak—telephonic contact, my English came above all from the poems and novels I had read.

Panic is fought, as we all know, with distilled beverages, and after a while I was calmer. Plus, I only had to speak a little in English, just a long greeting; the main event was the bilingual reading with Megan McDowell, who read excerpts in translation. That was the night I met Megan, with whom I had only exchanged a few emails, and I hadn't even known of the existence of Jessye, her twin sister. The two of them appeared suddenly and made me guess which one was Megan, and I guessed wrong. I asked Jessye what she did; she's a visual artist, but that night she told me that she was a translator like Megan, only from Chinese. For some twenty seconds I believed her; for twenty seconds I not only conceived of the existence of those two twin translators of different languages, but I even had time to get used to the idea. Emboldened by all these new friends, that night I didn't try in the slightest to speak well, and I'm sure I spoke badly and that precisely for that reason, it more or less worked.

In the following years I went back to New York a few times, always short visits for work, but always with the audacity of a tourist tattooed on my spirit. I think I could write a giant tome about those trips and never get bored, but of course I would bore everyone else. So instead I'll skip ahead to the chapter that starts in September of 2015, when I went to live in New York for a considerably longer time, thanks to a blessed grant to work at the Public Library. By that time I could communicate with anyone, as long as I accepted the unsettling absence of favorite words and the general lack of consistency: the impossibility of playing with tone, or of cracking jokes. That degradation was the price of speaking English daily with my fellow grant recipients. I spoke better if there was no one on the radar who understood Spanish: my English worked better if I gave free reign to my histrionic side.

During those first days I remember thinking—pretty optimistically—that I could use that chance to be, in English, a different person. I remember trying, even: to be a person who spoke less, for example. Because I speak slowly, but a lot. The feeling of having said too much (I mean literally: the annoying certainty that I've pronounced too many words) has been with me almost my whole life. I thought that in English I could be more direct, more solid, less tentative. Very soon, however, after just a couple of weeks, I was me again, or that precarious version of me (ever less precarious but ever more aware of my precariousness, which in some way reinforced or legitimated the precariousness). Very soon I wasn't translating myself, I mean: I simply operated with the words I had, which weren't so few but seemed so when I compared them with the ones I had in Spanish. The feeling I was imitating someone grew ever less funny, and often turned alarming. Not the imitation itself, but its condition of indeterminacy: I aspired to know, at the very least, who I was imitating.

4

I lived in Crown Heights, just steps from the Brooklyn Botanical Garden, in a spacious old apartment temporarily vacated by Bex Brian and Charles Siebert, a couple of writers who I knew very little but who were and still are the best friends of my great friend Francisco Goldman, so I had the feeling I knew them well.

In one of his many gestures of courtesy, Chuck had left a gift for me on his desk: a copy of his book *Wickerby*, a memoir set at the end of the eighties in that very apartment. "The book essentially recreates my thoughts on a September night, looking out at the neighborhood from the living room windows," Chuck told me in an email whose main subject was not *Wickerby*, but rather the function of some service that would allow him and Bex—as long as I didn't commit the fatal mistake of unplugging the modem in the main bedroom—to watch the Mets and the Giants live from Abu Dhabi.

Out of curiosity and a love of symmetry, I read *Wickerby* on the last night of September, when I had already spent a few weeks circulating through the apartment like an intruder. The protagonists of *Wickerby* are none other than Charles and Bex, but twenty years ago, when they were thirty-somethings. The story, from the start, is dramatic: Bex travels to a remote region of Africa, and Chuck stays in the Brooklyn apartment with Lucy the dog, and for a while all is well, but the months pass and Bex, giving no convincing reasons, indefinitely puts off her return. Chuck doesn't know what to do or what to think, so he decides to take Lucy on a trip; they go not to Africa but to Wickerby, which is the name of a run-down cabin in the woods, south of Quebec, where Bex used to go as a child.

Chuck's tone is colloquial and hospitable, but also at times strangely elliptical, as if he didn't want to tell the story, or as if he trusted too much in the reader's complicity. Or rather: as if he knew the only way to tell that story was by pretending he was talking to a silent and understanding friend—kind of like a first person that wants to be perceived as third. *Wickerby* is a romantic book in the most traditional sense: the character continuously projects himself into the bucolic Canadian vistas or the urban landscape of Crown Heights as if he is channeling into them his pain, his unease, his bewilderment.

Immediately after reading *Wickerby* I was struck by a certain sorrow, or an affectionate and confused feeling tied to those characters whom I suddenly knew too well. I felt that inhabiting their apartment—their scenery—was a strange luxury. Suddenly I cared about them; or, more precisely, I missed them: I would have loved for them to come home unexpectedly so I could talk to them for hours and offer Lucy some treats. From that feeling arose the idea or the impulse to translate Charles's book. I decided to translate *Wickerby* more or less for the same reason one decides to write a book: to do something, to stop thinking.

To translate a person is 'to translate a text that doesn't exist,' says Adam Phillips in a beautiful essay I read not long ago. The idea is more complex, because Phillips sets out to compare literary translation with therapy: if the therapist is a 'translator,' the patient, then, is a sort of text. But a person is not just one text, rather an infinite series, none of which could be considered the original; a book is, in the best of cases, the text that a person once was or wanted to be, but of course it's a multiple testament, ambiguous and full of meaning. The idea that we are untranslatable is, however, much more damaging than the idea that we are translatable. To suppose that no one can translate us is to renounce the plane of contact, to remove ourselves from the world, proud and cowering. But Chuck's trip to Wickerby was not an escape; losing himself in the forest that belonged to his wife, to his wife's childhood, was his tangled, painful way of translating her.

5

Every morning, over coffee, before leaving the house—because I felt that the translation had to be perpetrated right there: at that desk, in that apartment, in that neighborhood—I would translate one or two paragraphs of Chuck's book, and then I'd set off for the library, where I would read and take notes. After lunch I reserved a couple of hours to work on my own novel, which I had decided to write in English, though I didn't have the least intention of publishing it or even of showing it to anyone. Writing in English was more like part of the immersion method, so to speak, and it was also an arduous game of literacy that left me exposed to problems or dilemmas that I had more or less resolved in Spanish.

The novel really did matter to me, and so the whole time I worked on it I felt an inevitable stylistic frustration: the poverty of the rhythm, the scarcity of words—two words, three at most, for what in Spanish I had five or six or ten—paradoxically reconciled me with literature. My novel in English took paths that it never would have taken in Spanish. I felt like a guitarist forced to use only three notes, the first ones he'd ever learned. I like thinking back to those writing sessions, though at the time I suffered and was always on the verge of abandoning the novel. Toward the end of the day, when I wrote in Spanish, I felt again the pleasant sonorous exuberance, the inestimable joy of talking with my mouth full.

I wrote my bad novel in English thinking that later on I would translate it myself into Spanish, and then Megan would return it to its place of origin, the English language. And I translated Chuck's book imagining that at the same time, in Santiago, Megan herself was translating something of mine. I even came to imagine, indulgently, that it was all a comedy of switched countries, with a featured appearance by Jessye, the false Chinese translator who'd become a real Chinese translator, and whose presence created all kinds of misunderstandings: a deliciously stupid sitcom about two translator twins lost in Santiago or Beijing or New York or who knows where. By then I knew people who didn't speak a lick of Spanish but who had read my books in translation, which was flattering but also, sometimes, intimidating. I liked to imagine myself as Megan's front man: I had put my name to those books that really she had written, and my job was to play along and do everything possible not to awaken suspicion.

6

One morning I received an invitation to give a reading of my books in English. I know people who do everything they can to avoid public readings, and it strikes me as the most reasonable phobia in the world, but I love them, or at least I don't dislike them. Reading aloud is the only literary activity that—in Spanish, of course—feels almost completely comfortable, because I came of age doing poetry recitals, and through a process of hitting and missing I think I ended up learning to interpret a text, in the musical sense. In general I don't like it when they have actors perform readings instead of the writers (especially, of course, if they're bad actors). But reading Megan's translations as if they were mine was basically acting, imitating. And nor did I know which excerpts to read, because what I would read in Spanish wasn't necessarily—in the abstract, I mean—what I would read in English. That morning, planning to choose a few fragments to read, I stretched out on the sofa to read my books translated by Megan, which I already knew but had never reread, the same way I never reread my books in Spanish.

In her magnificent essay *This Little Art*, Kate Briggs insists on the 'novelesque' nature of literary translation. The famous suspension of disbelief that operates in the reading of a novel also functions in reading translation, and it takes on even more weight, because the question about what was actually said or written is always slightly suspended. The reader's pact is more sophisticated; when we read a translated novel it's more 'fictional' than a novel in our own language. When a translation is praised, what is meant is that it doesn't seem like a translation (except in the very infrequent case when the reviewer is fluent in the original language).

Asking a writer for an opinion of the translation of his book to a language he knows only partially is like asking a dog how the cat's food is going down. I thought Megan's translations were excellent, but I had no way of proving it, except for very subjective images. Every time I heard her read a text of mine out loud, starting on that first, long-past night of quickened blood, I had the vivid sense that she was reading a text entirely her own. The afternoon I spent reading Megan's translations, that impression became a certainty, as for long passages I forgot that I was the one who had written those books. Or to put it more exactly: for long passages I forgot that those words corresponded to something I had said/ written in another language. Sometimes the name of a place or a person returned me to reality, but the illusion did its thing and always returned.

I chose the excerpts to read in public, though the central problem remained: there was something essentially illegitimate in that reading, whose only interest was the link between the written word and the voice of the writer. For the text to work, I had to articulate or pronounce it creating the feeling that it was mine. And nor was I sure of the most intelligible pronunciation of certain words, especially certain vowels—those details that in a conversation don't matter, but that in a reading mark insurmountable differences in meaning. I asked my friend John Wray to read those fragments and I tried to sound like him, but John is good looking and taller than me and much blonder, so I felt like I was fifteen again, imitating those kids from the English school. Then I asked Megan for her interpretation over the phone, and I listened to those audio files a hundred times, and then, at the reading, before an audience that I think was very merciful, I tried to pronounce the words the way Megan would, and of course I must have sounded, in the best case, like a first-time actor trying out for a role that was too big for him.

By now there are a lot of people with whom I have only spoken English, and I like to think that I put together a language using the phrases they lent me or that I stole from them; that now, when I speak English, I imitate their voices, and from imitating them so much there are times, like in a Fernando Pessoa poem, when I feel like my pretend language is a language of my own, a way of speaking that is mine. And I suppose that dormant within the mutant I proudly call *my English,* there also lurk the ruckus of friends getting drunk and the erratic conversations with that asshole Chad and the letters that Emily Dickinson sent to the world and the poems by Donne and Auden and the songs of the summer and the *Seinfeld* episodes I know by heart. And the novel I wrote in English planning to never show to anyone and that these days I'm translating, amazed at how each English phrase multiplies by two or four in Spanish. And Chuck's book, of course: I suppose my English holds several phrases from that book that I never finished translating: I abandoned it with only the last chapter to go, the final eleven pages, I don't really know why. Surely it was so I'd have an excuse to go back to that apartment and settle in for a few hours until I finished translating the book its owner wrote.

7

My wife learned English by reading Harry Potter. At twelve years old, tired of waiting for the fourth novel in the series to be translated, she decided to read it in English. She got her hands on a copy that she read immediately, though it's more true to fact to say that her eyes passed over all the words and all the sentences on all the pages of the book, because she understood very little. She started it again right away, this time with the help of a dictionary. She wasn't interested in the English language, she was interested in *Harry Potter.*

I find on our shelves, camouflaged among manuals and encyclopedias, the copy that she read. It's an imposing hardcover in good condition, with a minimum of ten and a maximum of thirty words underlined on each one of its 752 pages. "I didn't read, I didn't eat, I didn't do anything but try to read that novel," she tells me. In a month she had finished it or finished it again, and along the way she had learned enough English to improvise a few spells or comment on a game of quidditch. Meanwhile, the Spanish edition of *Harry Potter and the Goblet of Fire* still hadn't appeared. She remembers asking, in the voice of a desperate teenager, "How can it take so long to translate a book?"

Jazmina went on reading in English and later majored in it at UNAM and then went to study in New York, where one afternoon, out of curiosity, she went to an event at the Public Library where I was giving a flawed but loquacious talk, and in the Q&A session afterward she raised her hand and asked me a question that neither of us remembers, but I do remember that her English sounded lovely—much better than mine, of course. I remember having sensed that English was her second language but I knew I could be wrong, and I also remember thinking while she spoke that her native language was Spanish and it was absurd for me to respond in English, but the event was in English, so we had to speak English.

I don't know if we're going quickly or slowly as we translate, now, *Little Labors*, the funny and brilliant essay by Rivka Galchen. It's the second book we've translated together. The first was a selection of non-fiction pieces by Daniel Alarcón—a very strange case, because Daniel's Spanish is very good but he has written almost all of his literary works in English, though they largely take place in Latin America, in a country remarkably similar to Peru. When he writes, Daniel translates into English the Peruvian that we tried to recover in the translation, as if we were writing out some kind of original.

When we were translating Daniel's chronicles, Jazmina was three months pregnant and we had just moved to Mexico City; everything seemed imposing and intense and decisive, and maybe it wasn't the best moment to set off on an uncertain adventure like working together for the first time. But it worked. Then Rivka Galchen's book appeared in our lives by chance, though it was guided chance: almost all the books we read about pregnancy and childcare were insufferable, moralising and heavy-handedly pedagogical, but we stumbled on this essay and found it wonderful and decided to translate it.

The solitude of the translator is complete, which makes translating together, shoulder to shoulder, so reasonable. And when I say reasonable, I mean that it is beautiful. I translate while Jazmina nurses, and she translates while the baby plays with his blind giraffe and with me. And when he falls asleep we translate together, compare versions, read aloud, correct, workshop. Rivka writes with wisdom and humour about experiences that we have just experienced or are experiencing now or will very soon experience, so the feeling that she is the one translating us is strong and frequent.

"I sometimes feel, as a mother, that there is no creature I better understand than my child," says Rivka, and then she thinks of those romantic comedies where the protagonists don't speak the same language but they still fall in love. But she also records the fear that soon, when her daughter learns to speak, the misunderstandings will begin, or that the real misunderstanding is the current feeling that they understand each other completely.

For now, at eight months old, my son strikes me as the most interesting person on the planet. Every morning I wake up around five-thirty, and he has already spent a while murmuring a kind of litany. Then comes a more defined contact: he focuses on me, looks at me, scratches at my cheek. It's his way of asking me to get this day started once and for all. He seems to know that these first two hours—the only ones fully given over to his mother's rest—are ones we'll spend alone, just the two of us, looking out the window at the half-dark, empty streets and playing with his books on the colored rug.

A couple of weeks ago he started to wave his left hand in greeting, though he doesn't only wave at people or his own reflection in the mirror or the silent TV: sometimes I think he also waves at the day or the sofa or a certain stain on the wall or at the solar system. Sometimes I have the impression that he speaks fluently, articulately, in a language I don't know; a language that has to change every day in order to go on existing. But I don't have the feeling of translating him, of having to translate him. Instead of encouraging him to imitate or assimilate my words, I'm the one who imitates his noises. Or rather I try to imitate them, because they're not easy and by now they are countless: sighs long and short, timid variations on the gasp, happy snorts, traditional babbles and others almost hummed, a sneeze-like laugh and another more like a giggle, and a long, enthusiastic raspberry. The thought that soon he'll leave behind that happy vanguard of sounds to adopt the conventions of human language brings on an anticipatory nostalgia in me. Even so, I'm pleased to announce here that the first word my son pronounced, a few weeks ago now, was the word *papa*. He says it all the time, it's the only word he says. He still has trouble, it's true, pronouncing the voiceless bilabial stop *p*, so that for now he replaces it with the voiced bilabial nasal *m*.

Rubén Martín Giráldez
Honor de Syntax Honours the Syntax

attempted translation by Diego Gerard ***

To describe the translator as a *medium* is not to say anything particularly radical. One could also describe the translator as a form of *sheath*. Now, knowing that this text is to be translated from the Spanish into the English, we will allow the translator (not me, a different one, the one dealing with my spectre (and spectrum)) to judge whether he will take 'sheath' to mean a 'scabbard for a sword' or 'a pod that recoats the ultra-body, substituting its host.'[2] By beginning with a tiny amount of innocence/unwariness and another small semblance of ineffectiveness/ill will, I have somehow formulated two different positions with two distinct functional meanings: in the first we continue within the semantic field of the *medium*, of possession, of conduction, definitively; and in the second we are still talking about a covering, a jacket, a container, an insulation.

To attempt uniting them both: the translator is a sword-swallower: a sheath that compromises its own integrity. This might seem an exaggerated *diversion* (*rodeo* in Spanish), aberrant even, to reel-in Kate Briggs' string of ideas, but what do you want me to do?

From here on in, unless I have miscalculated, my translator is engaged in decisions and elisions which I can only guess the nature of. And so, I am in the same position as you: a mere spectator. Yet I can almost certainly deduce that at the end of the previous paragraph he (the editor) found himself obliged to insert a footnote explain-

---

*** The translator thinks of translation as a *failed art* and / or *trying to hold a handful of sand.*

2. Image derived from the film *Invasion of the Body Snatchers* (1956), directed by Don Siegel and remade in 1978 by Philip Kaufman, where alien plant spores have fallen from space and grown into seed pods, each one capable of reproducing a duplicate/replacement version of each human.

ing the forced, clumsy, rickety play of Spanish words and musical references. Perhaps the Spanish word for *sheath* (vaina) produces the same dilemmas as in English, that is, that *it leads* (*dar pie* in Spanish) to a complete misunderstanding and not to the insertion of a new *footnote* (*nota al pie*). In fact, I think it's almost inevitable that we will lose the thread of this new word game between 'to lead' and 'footnote'. And so on and so on, interminably.

In any case, if you lose this book, know that, for practical effects, I am your spare copy. Few times have I been more conscious of it than during the translation of *This Little Art*.

> 'Here I am writing in English (so I am). Now I am writing in French (no, and this is the problem: no you're not).'[3]

We can say that in this case the translator's sheath appears to be figured typographically in the form of brackets (any implied insolence is fully intentional!) And in my translation,[4] my sheaths exist within Briggs' sheaths (my apologies). In Briggs' book, in my work within Kate Briggs' book, I have found an alibi for doing my duty as a translator, my own contagious criterion. I can explain this to you while I write a 'Translator's Note' for the ferocious and fertile novel by Pierre Guyotat *Éden, Éden, Éden*, published in 1970 by Gallimard; *Edén, Edén, Edén*, in Spanish, published by Malas Tierras; *Eden, Eden, Eden* in English, translated by Graham Fox for Creation Books.

---

3. Kate Briggs, *This Little Art*, p. 22, Fitzcarraldo Editions, London 2017

4. In his Spanish version, by the publishing house Jekyll & Jill, Rubén Martín Giráldez adds information between square brackets::
"Aquí estoy escribiendo en inglés (yo también, [en el caso de que esto que digo no esté ya, a su vez, traducido a otro idioma]). Ahora estoy escribiendo en francés (no, y ese es el problema: no estás escribiendo en francés)."

'In fact, all things are made from other things, and all things, and all people, have precedents, and so we are all translations – aren't we? – in one way or another'.

Translator's Note

One moment. I'd like to warn you that I have disparaged the excessively corny, flowery and bashful tone in all subsequent versions, but I think it's more useful to go through the humiliation of the original:

Translator's Note

> ... and excuse, an alibi, a plea, even (the copulative conjunctions are mine). I write this note as I build a set of criteria with the editors that we hope will do justice to *Éden, Éden, Éden*. It seems that the best option is to remain attached to (or to represent the theatric act of detaching from) the original, to shatter the formulas that tend to become artificial when translating and thus open up the possibility of naturalness or the most contiguous possible truth. This time, it seems of the utmost importance to respect phonetics.

I can't see it clearly. We begin with homophony and end up riming at crosscurrent. Let's start again.

Another reason for writing this note is that at the end, the tentativeness of homophony reveals itself as infantile and a sense of useful unease emerges, a false and unearned maturity. ("The chance it offers of becoming-expert, becoming-linguistically and culturally competent, becoming-critical, becoming-intimate, be coming a better—or, if not a better [...]—then certainly a different reader and writer")[5]. The need to arrive somewhere, to not abandon the text at page 90, once we have already returned at least seven times to each word to locate it and dislocate it and locate it again. I rewrite:

Translator's Note

I'm aware that it's neither illicit to ask you to read this translation with a gigantic, colossal, perpetual *sic* between brackets nor that you are forced to wander through labyrinths of extreme philology.

For this note I have also considered assembling my own monster from scraps, tangents and contradictory criteria. For example, when the French word 'reins' did not seem to acquire the same concept in terms of image, graphical symbol and sound. Instead I sought other possibilities—*riñonada, riñones, lumbares, lomo, espinazo, rabadilla*—or contemplated the option of using the obsolete 'renglada'. Or simply saying 'cintura' but the *cintura* (waist) is not as erotic in the same way as *lomo bajo* (lower back)—the *llom de dos colors*, as we say in Catalan, 'a piece of meat a bit higher towards the pig's head'. If we call everything by the same name, how will we give each part its proper due? It's a matter of tact, as Briggs says as she translates Barthes:

'Tact: the art of not treating all things in the same way. Of treating what appears to be the same as though different.'

Translating *This Little Art* has certainly affected me, has provoked in me an affection, has made me lost, a vaporous drool of psycho-kinetic energy.

---

5. Kate Briggs, *This Little Art*, p. 207, Fitzcarraldo Editions, London 2017

The pharsalia** of it all obliges me to pose Briggsian questions to Rubenian faltering: What can a writer do with Guyotat's work if not translate it? What can a writer do to translate it? How will a writer translate it? How would a writer even dare to translate Guyotat? (in the sense of committing an 'imprudence' and of 'daring' simultaneously) Is he still a writer after translating Guyotat? (in the sense of 'after committing the imprudence with success' and 'after committing the imprudence and messing it up' simultaneously) How could a writer and a Guyotat reader himself avoid being his translator and for how long? He could avoid it in public. He could elude that responsibility (and the risk) or consider that the responsible thing is not to be found guilty of an incorrect translation. Do correct translations even exist?

'(If you don't want to do mistakes, don't attempt translations)'

And further ahead, more alibis for a translator with the clipped ears of a Doberman:

'The point is, reading is its own work; it does its own extraordinary work. But it is not writing. It is not yet, not already, not practically writing.'

To write is to have read. But should I write translations?

'It is very fraught, this question of who can be trusted with the work of representing the speech, the writing, the work of someone else: who is learned enough, who is experienced enough, who is sensitive and careful enough. The question

---

** "farsalia" in Spanish: a word that to the translator is loaded with the word "farza" (farce) in the context of the sentence in Spanish. Yet another play of words that trickles away while translating—more rebellious grains of sand.

becomes more difficult still when we consider the uneven dynamics of any translation relation, and especially the English-language translator's real power.'

Me the autodidact thinks/fears the moment of meeting Kate Briggs, when she notices my pronunciation and my presumable macaronic tone while the voice of reason croons:

'Con tanto inglé que tú sabía,
Bito Manué,
con tanto inglé, no sabe ahora
desí ye.'*[6]

The responsibility, the danger of over-writing, the sliding jigsaw, the book that effaces itself or deforms itself when read twice, like running a hand over a short-haired rug. Like in Paul Celan's verse 'Gras, auseinander geschrieben', 'Written Asunder' in English, of which I know two different translations into the Spanish: 'hierba, separadamente escrita' and 'hierba, escrita una fuera de la otra.'[7] 'Writing Written' say Barthes-Briggs, 'Twice Written; the second time by her [the translator]'.

---

* The best case yet of 'the untranslatable' in a text about translation and its ontological flaws—the most dangerous of land-mines scattered throughout these pages.

6. From Emilio Grenet Sánchez's *Tú No Sabe Inglé*, part of Sánchez's research and journey through the musical creation of the early twentieth century in Cuba.

7. The first by José Luis Reina Palazón and the second by Jesús Munárriz.

The talented ventriloquist is the most perverse, the one whose lips move the least, the one who knows how to 'project the voice' (a technique that, the experts note, does not really exist, and that has more to do with misdirecting attention by way of gesture, posture and which direction they are looking). The translator can drink a glass of water while translating a phrase; the ventriloquist's mouth barely makes contact with the glass.

> 'Come here, sit down and attend for a while to this, to someone else's work, and let's see what that does. ('One of the ways to get around the confines of one's *identity* as one produces expository prose,' writes Spivak, 'is to work at someone else's title, as one works with a language that belongs to many others. This after all, is one of the seductions of translating.')'

Okay, okay, this is all well and good, but what would a book in my place do? And two?

Sophie Collins
The Joy of Translation

In November 2018, I saw Kate Briggs give a talk to students at the Glasgow School of Art. Citing Linda Alcoff's 'The Problem of Speaking for Others', she spoke honestly and eloquently about the imposter syndrome translating Roland Barthes has engendered in her, about how she attempts to harness the ensuing shame and embarrassment in order to make something valuable. In her case, this something valuable was, in addition to her translations themselves, her book on translation, *This Little Art*, as well as, of course, the very lecture I was watching her deliver.

As Briggs spoke, I felt seen. In literary contexts, the realities and physical demands of the practice of translation are often hidden from view, cloaked in metaphor. Any so-called negative emotions related to the experience of translating are thus also overlooked, though they have often been at the front of my mind.

* * *

The joy of translation. It's a phrase I have come across again and again. The first time I heard it, it provoked in me a kind of awe; I wished very much to be that joyful person, that translator experiencing an uncorrupted sense of singing tunefully in key with the source text.

I now experience the same phrase as alienating, a refrain which reflects my insecurities by underlining the fact that I never have or will be able to translate without a certain self-awareness. Increasingly, however, I know this disaffection to be a source of strength and, ultimately, of creativity.

* *

As an infant, poet and translator Don Mee Choi's family was forced to leave South Korea for Hong Kong during the former's military dictatorship following the May 16 coup, in which Park Chung Hee and the Military Revolutionary Committee (as backed by US military forces) took control of the state from North Korea. Later, as a teenager, she moved – alone – to the US. Asked in a recent interview to name 'the greatest joy' of translating from Korean to English, Choi responded,

> I am terrified of English. And because I have lived outside of South Korea for a long time, I've become a foreigner to Korean as well. In other words, I am a failure of language in general. So joy does not come to mind easily when I think about translating from Korean to English. I also associate joy with 'Joy of this and that' I saw and heard everywhere when I first came to [the US], including green-coloured JOY detergent. It was the first dish soap I used after my arrival. I wondered, even in my state of devastation having just separated from my family, why this nation was so obsessed with joy when it causes so much misery all over the world.

Here Choi consolidates an understanding of 'joy' as a conformist trope, a verbal deposit of the imperial mindset, so ubiquitous in Anglophone countries as to be used to sell washing-up liquid.

In *The Promise of Happiness*, Sara Ahmed writes of the 'critique of happiness as an affirmative gesture', a statement which might, on first reading, appear somewhat paradoxical. But what Ahmed is in fact proposing is that such a critique represents possibility because that which we have come to accept or recognise as 'happiness' is merely a kind of cultural 'promise' tendered 'for having the right associations'. 'In wishing for happiness,' she writes, 'we wish to be associated with happiness, which means to be associated with its associations.' Such associations, suggests Ahmed, are represented by the dominant values of a given society, and so the individual's search for happiness is often simply the gradual acquiescence to dominant mores, including the desire for heteronormative relationships, for children, for property.

The joy of translation. To state anything to the contrary is to be made to feel ashamed. Like Choi, Ahmed links her formulation of joy or 'happiness' to the domestic realm, referencing Betty Friedan's debunking of the myth of 'the happy American housewife' in *The Feminine Mystique*:

> What lies behind this image [writes Ahmed] bursts through, like a boil, exposing an infection underneath her beaming smile. ... The happy housewife is a fantasy figure that erases the signs of labour under the sign of happiness. The claim that women are happy and that this happiness is behind the work they do functions to justify gendered forms of labour, not as a product of nature, law or duty, but as an expression of a collective wish and desire. How better to justify an unequal distribution of labour than to say that such labour makes people happy? How better to secure consent to unpaid or poorly paid labour than to describe such consent as the origin of good feeling.

'Erasing the signs of labour under the sign of happiness': this perfect phrase of Ahmed's encapsulates what I'm trying to express, namely that *the joy of translation* is troubling not because I have an issue with its fundamental proposition, i.e. that translation is or can be enjoyable, but that the common application of this phrase reduces its affect to a sign, one that is in some way intended to justify the lack of artistic recognition and inequitable pay that translators still receive.

* * *

The gendered language of translation and its effects on perceptions of the practice have been well-documented. In *Gender in Translation*, Sherry Simon draws lines between women and translators as having historically represented 'the weaker figures in their respective hierarchies', linking such perceptions to power dynamics and biological reproduction.

In *Gender and the Metaphorics of Translation*, Lori Chamberlain adds that such metaphors are consolidated by the dominance of capitalist beliefs, given that translations have, like 'conventional representations of women', been determined by 'a cultural ambivalence about the possibility of a woman artist and about the status of a woman's "work"'.

Gendered cultural models that enable claims such as the infamous 'there are no great women artists' differentiate between 'productive' and 'reproductive' work, presenting 'originality or creativity in terms of paternity and authority' and 'relegating the figure of the female to a variety of secondary roles'.

* * *

Here is my confession: my translating (from the Dutch) evokes feelings of uncertainty and self-consciousness, and – perhaps more frequently than might be imagined – frustration, break-down. Sometimes I feel fulfilled and stimulated by the interaction; at other times it exacerbates my persisting imposter syndrome, the uneasy sense that, having now lived in the UK continuously for a decade, I no longer have a stake or claim in the language and culture that fostered me for fourteen years during the most influential stage of life, from childhood into young adulthood.

Affect proliferates during translation, and enjoyment or pleasure might manifest at some point during, or on either side of, it, but any joy in the process is tied to – is inextricable from – these negative affects.

'Revolutionary forms of political consciousness,' says Ahmed, 'involve heightening our awareness of just how much there is to be unhappy about. Given that the desire for happiness can cover signs of its negation, a revolutionary politics has to work hard to stay proximate to unhappiness.'

Kate Briggs & Arno Renken
Notes on the Table /
Notes autour de la table

If a translation is like a table, it is like Robinson Crusoe's: a rectangular thing, imported in its conception from elsewhere, but made again for the first time, and solely with the available materials, on this small round island.

La table de Robinson : tout à la fois importée et réinventée – autrement dit, table traduite. Là-bas, sur cette île, « translation is like a table » est réversible. La table de Robinson est aussi comme une traduction.

(Robinson's table: all together imported and reinvented – in other words, a table translated. Over there, on such an island, 'translation is like a table' is reversible. Robinson's table is also like a translation.)

La table-traduction promet les joies de l'écriture et des saveurs... « And now I began to apply myself to make such necessary things as I found I most wanted, particularly a chair and a table; for without these I was not able to enjoy the few comforts I had in the world; I could not write or eat, or do several things with so much pleasure without a table. »

(The table-translation promises the pleasures of writing and eating, tasting... 'And now I began to apply myself to make such necessary things as I found I most wanted, particularly a chair and a table; for without these I was not able to enjoy the few comforts I had in the world; I could not write or eat, or do several things with so much pleasure without a table.')

... et la table-traduction est l'événement de rencontres : « [...] and having set a table there for them, I sat down and ate my dinner also with them; and, as well as I could, cheered them and encouraged them, Friday being my interpreter, especially to his father, and indeed to the Spaniard too; for the Spaniard spoke the language of the savages pretty well. »

(and the table-translation is the chance for encounters: '[...] and having set a table there for them, I sat down and ate my dinner also with them; and, as well as I could, cheered them and encouraged them, Friday being my interpreter, especially to his father, and indeed to the Spaniard too; for the Spaniard spoke the language of the savages pretty well.')

If a translation is like Robinson Crusoe's table, then it consists of a flat slab-like top braced by legs and other (normally, but not always, visible) supports.

Et si, réciproquement, la table de Robinson est comme une traduction – un étrangement de l'île par ses propres matériaux réassemblés, disparition d'un arbre et invention d'une échappée en creux d'elle-même – alors l'île devient autre chose. En ce minuscule point, l'île dérive, embarque ou flotte.

(And if Robinson's table is, reciprocally, like a translation – an estrangement of the island by means of its own reassembled materials, felling a tree and inventing an escape from within itself – then the island becomes something else. In this tiny respect, the island drifts, becomes unmoored, it floats.)

But if a translation is like any table – or, let's say, like every table – then it will have known and be open to different kinds of making (for example, both its initial assemblage and its later repeated setting). And when a translation is like this kind of every-table, then it is also, etymologically speaking, a plate, a meal, an offering.

En français (est-ce aussi le cas en anglais ?), le mot « table » rend indécises les limites de son objet. « Table » désigne certes cette chose identifiable, formée d'un plateau et de pieds (où sont ces jambes, legs, que tu lui attribues, ou que ta langue lui lègue ?). Mais comme pour accueillir ses abords, le mot « table » désigne également ce qui entoure immédiatement son objet : la nourriture que le meuble porte (« les plaisirs de la table ») ou les personnes qui partagent le repas.

(In French (is it also the case in English?) the word 'table' rubs at the limits of its object. Yes, 'table' designates that identifiable thing, composed of a top and feet (Where are these legs, *legs*, that you attribute to it – or that your language bequeaths it?). But as if it were playing host to, welcoming in its surroundings, the word 'table' also designates what is most proximate to its object: the food that the piece of furniture bears ('the pleasures of the table') or the people who are sharing the meal.)

Si la traduction est comme une table, elle rend incertains les contours de ce qu'elle relie, et à commencer ceux des mots eux-mêmes : quand commence une traduction et quand finit-elle ? Et quand « table » cesse d'être un mot de ta langue et devient « table » dans la mienne ?

(If translation is like a table, it makes the contours of what it holds together uncertain, undecidable, starting with the borders of words themselves: when does a translation begin and when does it end? And when does 'table' cease to be a word in your language become 'table' in mine?)

I would add: where does it begin – and where does it end? Where are the edges of the languages we claim as our own? Or the centres?

But I write this in English.

If translation is like a table, then, following Hannah Arendt, it is a thing located between those able to sit at it. A common thing in-between that separates and relates at the same time.

La traduction serait comme une table (et réciproquement peut-être) en ce qu'elle forme un entre-deux qui rassemble et sépare en même temps. Mais il n'y a pas que le vis-à-vis, l'ici et le là-bas ; il y a aussi le dessus et le dessous de la table. Ici, la table forme l'interface entre le caché et le manifeste. De nombreuses expressions francophones en attestent : on joue cartes sur table lorsqu'on ne dissimule rien, on paye des dessous de table lorsqu'on veut corrompre. Au-delà des enjeux moraux, une table expose et recouvre.

(A translation would be like a table (and vice versa, perhaps) insofar as it forms a between that gathers and separates at the same time. But there are not only the two sides, the here and the over there, there is also the atop and the underneath of the table. Here, the table forms the interface between the hidden and the manifest. Many francophone sayings bear this out: we put our cards on the table when we have nothing to hide, we pay, in French, not just under but literally with the underside of the table when we're doing a dodgy deal. Beyond the moral questions, a table exposes and covers over.)

Si la traduction est comme une table, elle rassemble tant par ce qu'elle dit que par ce qu'elle tait. Elle relie et sépare et elle donne à lire et donne à ne pas lire.

(If translation is like a table, it gathers together as much by way of what it says as by what it withholds. It relates and separates and it opens up to reading and to not reading, to what can be read and what is not to be read.)

C'est l'attention merveilleuse et magique par laquelle s'ouvre This Little Art : que par la traduction les personnages peuvent parler une langue dans laquelle nous ne lisons pas leurs paroles, qu'ils peuvent parler une langue en en taisant une autre.

(This is the marvelous and magic perception which opens This Little Art: that by means of translation characters can speak a language in which we don't read what they say, that they can speak one language by silencing another.)

I could tell you, my friend, that I'm writing in French, or Dutch, or Japanese, or any one of the languages I can't write or speak. And the fiction layered on by translation, like a laquer surface onto a table – very thin, sometimes imperceptible – would make it not matter. In order to continue reading, continue engaging, you would accept the conceit in the way you would accept it if I told you a character's hair was brown. And you would read:

If a translation is like a table, then it is either, or can be alternately, the thing itself and the configuration of persons, separations and relations around it.

The word Arendt used was Tisch.

When I write that a translation is like a table, I am using two nouns that belong, undecidably, to English and French. To either English or French. Which could mean: to neither (entirely) English nor French. Et pourtant, quelle langue rend possible cette coexistence dans les deux langues ? Quelle langue saurait en faire l'expérience ?

(And yet, which language makes possible this co-existence within the two languages? In which language is it possible to experience it?)

Il me semble que ce ne pourrait être que la langue abstraite du dictionnaire. Mais considérée depuis ma langue, la coexistence ressemble plus à celle des figures réversibles : le canard-lapin n'est jamais simultanément un canardlapin. Impossible de percevoir les deux animaux en même temps. Pour voir, sous les 'mêmes' traits, l'un ou l'autre des animaux, je dois occulter l'autre : chasser le lapin pour voir le canard, chasser le canard pour voir le lapin.

(It seems to me that it could only be the abstract language of the dictionary. But considered from the perspective of my own language, the co-existence looks more like one of those reversible pictures: the duck-rabbit is never simultaneously a duckrabbit. It's not possible to see both animals at the same time. To see, in the 'same' lines, the one or other, I have to occult one of them: chase away the rabbit to see the duck, disappear the duck to see the rabbit).

Puis-je dire « table » ou « translation » à la fois en anglais ou en français ? Ou le dire en français serait-il productivement le taire en anglais ? Et ce geste de taire activement, n'est-il pas déjà traduire « table » par « table » ou « translation » par « translation » ?

(Can I say 'table' or 'translation' at the same time in English or in French? Or would to say it in French be to productively silence it in English? And this gesture of active silencing, is it not already to translate 'table' by 'table' or 'translation' by 'translation'?)

Peut-être est-ce cela que, plus haut, illustrait le dessous de table.

(Perhaps it's this that, as above, would illustrate the underside of the table.)

In French as in English, translation describes a function that moves an object a certain distance. The object is not altered in any other way. It is not rotated, reflected or re-sized.

Si la traduction est aussi comme le dessous d'une table, « a function that moves an object a certain distance. The object is not altered in any other way. It is not rotated, reflected or re-sized » n'est pas la définition du mot français, mais la traduction de sa définition. Elle tait de manière à ce que je puisse en deviner le silence, que jamais, en français, je ne décrirais translation ainsi.

(If translation is also like the underside or neath of a table, 'a function that moves an object a certain distance. The object is not altered in any other way. It is not rotated, reflected or re-sized' is not the definition of the French word, but the translation of its definition. It silences in such a way that I am able to guess the silence of it: the fact that never, in French, would I describe translation in this way.)

The words Arendt used were first Tisch and then table.

Et aussi, les mots qui se sont d'abord soustraits à Arendt étaient table puis Tisch.

(And what is more, the first words to be taken away from Arendt were table then Tisch.)

If I am attached to thinking of a translation as a kind of table, it is because I refuse to lose sight of translation as a means of making things in the world – of making new things in the world that did not exist in this exact way before. New things made on the basis of and closely related to existing things, where there will have been rotation, reflection, re-scaling, alteration. Books, but not only books, with their own material beings and styles of presence. New things to act on their own terms (for better or worse): plates, meals, offerings.

Je pense à cette si belle et énigmatique phrase de Carl Andre : « a thing is a hole in a thing it is not. » Il me semble qu'elle s'attache essentiellement à notre attention : à cette possibilité d'une attention réciproque ou réversible (comme le canard-lapin, le dessus-dessous de la table, la table-relation/table-séparation ou, pour notre texte, la table-traduction). Devant une œuvre de Carl Andre, je peux voir comment elle forme l'espace ; je peux voir aussi, quoique pas en même temps, combien elle troue ou interrompt l'espace sinon vide. Devant la table de Robinson, Vendredi a peut-être aussi vu l'absence de l'arbre qui la constitue.

(I'm thinking of that beautiful and enigmatic sentence from Carl Andre: 'a thing is a hole in a thing that it is not'. It seems to me that this essentially has to do with our attention: with this possibility of a reciprocal or reversible form of attention (like the duck-rabbit, the under-topside of the table, the table-relation/table-separation or, for our text, the table-translation). Standing before a work by Carl Andre, I can see how it shapes space; I can also see, although not at the same time the degree to which it holes or interrupts space that is otherwise empty. Standing before Robinson's table, maybe Friday also saw the absence of the tree that made it.)

Si la traduction est comme une table sur laquelle sont posés deux livres – peut-être Robinson Crusoe et sa traduction Robinson Crusoé – les deux sont là, faits dans le monde, faits du monde, ajouts. Si la traduction est comme une table, elle est comme cette table. J'y écris en français des mots que tu liras et écriras en anglais. J'y lis déjà la soustraction de ce qu'ils seront lorsqu'ils vivront là-bas, dans ta langue.

(If translation is like a table on which we have two books – maybe Robinson Crusoe and its translation Robinson Crusoé – both are there, things in the world, made of the world, additions. If translation is like a table, it is like that table. I write there in French words that you will read and write in English. Already, I read there the subtraction of what they will become when they live over with you, in your language.)

Mais sur cette table qu'est la traduction, à laquelle nous sommes invités à lire et à goûter, les livres marquent en creux l'absence de l'autre. Une minuscule marque « ´ » signe leur émancipation réciproque et, comme pour table/table ou translation/translation, embarquée dans la relation, je lirai, en creux des lignes, l'échappée joyeuse des lignes de l'autre.

(But on that table, this table, that is translation, on the surface of which we are invited to read and to partake, the books are each marked within themselves by the absence of the book they are not. A tiny sign –the accent on the é – authorises their emancipation from each other and, as for table/table or translation/translation, now their relating has begun, I read, in between the lines of the one book, the joyous escape of the lines from the other.)

Have I ever told you how much I love hearing French speakers pronounce the title of Defoe's novel? The emphasis falls so differently. Lift, lift, land: Ro-bin-son. Then: desperate (happy?) shipwreck: Cruise-away.

By convention I call the titular character Robinson Crusoe. But when I say the name out loud, in my formality, I can sometimes hear what I can't say: the sound of you calling him more casually, Robinson. You are on first name terms. As though, reading the book in French, you knew him better.

La traduction aura été comme ces tables sur laquelle j'écris et sur laquelle tu écris, à mille kilomètres d'ici. Nos textes ne s'y cumulent pas, ils y convivent.

Translation will have been.

Translation will have always been like these tables that I write on and you write on, that I am right now writing on (or at) and that you are right now writing on (or at) a thousand kilometers from here. Our texts don't accumulate, they don't cancel out or make up (for) each other. They co-exist, contiguously, on that table-plane. They live there apart together.

Renee Gladman
Untitled
(Translation Not-Knowing)

I began the day thinking how we can go from knowing to not-knowing in an instant; we can go from knowing to not-knowing back to knowing in the length of an instant; across an instant, we can take what we know and turn it into not-knowing and then we can know the not-knowing. It could be an instant, no longer than that stretch from *a* to *b* or that pause following the equal sign, the breath after the comma, that kind of instant where the light takes over the day, illuminates the whole expanse of your breathing and sets you on a path to glory and then, in the space of a comma, clouds come and cover and suddenly it's a very ordinary day, no glory in sight, and just as you begin to turn your mind toward some sleepy activity—not yet doing it but making its duration possible in your mind—the sun returns, the sky clears and you can see a sliver of the moon in broad daylight. You can go from knowing to not-knowing just as quickly as you can go from not-knowing to knowing, even though the thing you are now knowing came directly from what you hadn't known: you didn't know it because it first wasn't real; it wasn't anything, it was fiction. Fiction is a category of not-knowing; you walked proudly through it. But not-knowing doesn't last as long as knowing and that's why you tried to not-know for as long as you could and threw all these things in your path so that your path to knowing was full of things that made you confused and sleepy. I put something in front of my not-knowing; it was a line made of a blue pastel stick. I drew the line then pulled my finger through it. I wrote *ppp* at its bottom right corner to put sound to my not-knowing. I wanted it to be very soft. I wanted the moment to last as long as it could, so drew a deep orange line above the blue and ran my finger through it. I didn't know what I was doing with the not-knowing, it was almost as if I wanted to make the not-knowing look like knowing so that I could know it. In that moment I wanted to know not-knowing. I made an equation: *dv something something*, I wrote; *c* parenthesis *r* close parenthesis, I wrote. I drew a line in ink, then wrote *ppp* beneath the swiped-through blue and orange lines. I turned the orange and blue from lines into sectors, into veils. I wrote x then squared it. I placed next to it dv. I put dv in parentheses, then squared it, too. I was performing knowing on the not-knowing within the blurry veil of orange and blue; I wrote *ppp* to make it quiet. I was trying to get to a place where the instant I realised I was not-knowing, my not-knowing changed. It got louder, then quiet. I wanted math to be about how not-knowing had a shape and then I wanted the shape to have something like a cloak you could put over it and place inside a fiction. It would walk around your fiction and no one would know that it was math underneath, but a math about something that was categorically outside the realm of knowing but still known because it was math or looked like math. You could write something that looked like something else, that said it was something else while not looking like it; you could write something earnest that tried to say clearly that it was something looking at something else. You could write something else. You could sleep. You could add *vln* to your math then *dv* then *ppp*. I drew a thin diagonal line in white ink and put an arrow at its end. I return to the origin of that line and along its left side, moving incrementally upward, I began making short perpendicular lines extending from it, like arm hairs standing on end; halfway up I stopped, and returned again to the origin of the diagonal but now moved to the other side of the perpendicular lines; I drew another diagonal line, closing off the shorter, choppy ones. Two long beautiful, sharp lines drawn in white ink, connected by many measured, short perpendicular lines that carried halfway up the two lines, both diagonals ending with arrows. I finished the equation with a long line extending perpendicularly from the first diagonal line, but on its right side, with no arrow, disappearing into the veil, the blank space of the black sheet upon which something else had become something, in which something not-known was getting quickly caught up in something known.

CONTRIBUTORS'
BIOGRAPHIES

Paul Becker is a writer and painter based in Stockholm. In 2017 he published *Choreography*/Coreografia, a fiction set within a RW Fassbinder film, with *Juan de la Cosa/John of the Thing*. For the past four years he has been compiling an online, collective, ekphrastic novel *The Kink in the Arc*, with over seventy collaborating artists and writers.

Kate Briggs is a writer and translator based in Rotterdam, NL. Recent work includes *This Little Art*, published in 2017 by Fitzcarraldo Editions and *Entertaining Ideas (a short essay on "writing backwards" and Elizabeth Jane Howard's The Long View)* published in 2019 by Ma Bibliothèque. She is completing a novel-essay about the novel, titled *The Long Form*, which is forthcoming with Fitzcarraldo Editions.

Daniela Cascella is a writer whose work is centred on a longstanding study of the relationship between sound, voice, and literature. Her books, texts, scripts for spoken word articulate tensions and points of contact between the sonic and the literary, and propose a range of approaches to creative-critical writing through experiments with form and voice.

Sophie Collins grew up in Bergen, North Holland, and now lives in Glasgow. She is the author of *Who Is Mary Sue?* (Faber, 2018) and *small white monkeys* (Book Works, 2017), and the editor of *Currently & Emotion* (Test Centre, 2016), an anthology of contemporary poetry translations; a sequel, *Intimacy*, is forthcoming. She is a Fellow of the Royal Society of Literature and a Lecturer at the University of Glasgow. She is the translator, from the Dutch, of Lieke Marsman's *The Following Scan Will Last Five Minutes* (Pavilion, 2019). She is currently translating Marsman's novel, *The Opposite of a Person* (Daunt Books, 2022), as well as working on new poetry and a text on love, affect and fiction.

Renee Gladman is a poet, novelist, essayist and artist. She has published, amongst other books, the Ravicka series (four novel that appeared between 2010 and 2017), the crime novel *Morelia* (2019) and the monograph of drawings *Prose Architectures* (2017).

Nadia Hebson is an artist and educator. She uses painting, objects, large scale prints, apparel and text, to explore the work and biographies of older colleagues, including: American painter Christina Ramberg, British painters Winifred Knights and Marion Adnams and most recently, Dora Gordine as part of the Dorich House Museum Studio Residency. Exhibitions and commissions include *Gravidity & Parity &*, Hatton Gallery, Newcastle upon Tyne; *one on one: on skills*, The Contemporary Art Museum of Estonia, EKKM, Tallinn; *I See You Man*, Gallery Celine, Glasgow; *Alpha Adieu*, Museum of Contemporary Art Antwerp and *Choreography*, Arcade, London. In 2014 with AND Public she published MODA WK: Work in response to the paintings, drawings, correspondence, clothing and interior design of Winifred Knights (an expanded legacy). In 2017, with Hana Leaper she co-convened the conference, *Making Women's Art Matter*, at the Paul Mellon Centre, London.

Rubén Martín Giráldez is the translator of writers such as Kate Briggs, Angela Carter, Ted Chiang, Bruce Bégout, Pierre Guyotat or Eimear McBride. He has published two novels (*Magistral* and *Menos joven*) and some farcical essays about the likes of Ben Marcus and Thomas Pynchon.

Arno Renken teaches creative writing and literary translation at the University of the Arts Bern-HKB. His interests include theories of translation, the relations between philosophy and literature, research and creation, and questions of foreignness and exile. He is the author of *Babel heureuse. Pour lire la traduction* (Van Dieren, Paris, 2012) and initiator of a major interdisciplinary research project titled *Traduction / Relation*.

Alejandro Zambra is the author, amongst other books, of *Bonsái* (2006), *La vida privada de los árboles* (2007), *Formas de volver a casa* (2011), *Mis documentos* (2013), *Facsímil* (2014), *Tema libre* (2019) and *Poeta chileno* (2020). His work has been translated in more than twenty languages.

A Table Made Again for the First Time
On Kate Briggs' This Little Art

A table made again for the first time was initially presented as a talk, a book launch, a performance and screenings at Bureau des Réalités (Brussels) on 9, 11 & 12 September 2018. The overall project was dedicated to the idea of translation, both on the written page and in the exhibition space.

Published by Juan de la Cosa / John of the Thing

Editors Paul Becker and Francesco Pedraglio

Contributors
Paul Becker, Kate Briggs, Daniela Cascella, Sophie Collins,
Renee Gladman, Nadia Hebson, Rubén Martín Giráldez, Arno Renken,
Alejandro Zambra

Typesetting and formatting Carla Valdivia, Leonel Salguero at Studio Katsu

Printing Offset Rebosán

First edition 2021

Print run 750 copies

This publication was made possible thanks to the generous support of the Arts Council England and Bureau des Réalités (Brussels).

ISBN 978-0-9935229-5-6